Callan Uncovered 2

More 'Missing' Files

This second volume of 'lost' fiction featuring the iconic British spy David Callan comprises 15 short stories unseen since they were first published in the *Sunday Express* in 1970-72 plus a special 'Get Callan' background file prepared by James Mitchell for the *TV Times* to promote the third series of the hit television series *Callan* in 1970. In addition, there are two scripts of lost TV episodes for which no recordings are known to exist - *Goodness Burns Too Bright* (from 1967) and *Blackmailers Should Be Discouraged* (from 1969) – which have been reconstructed by editor Mike Ripley.

James William Mitchell (1926–2002) was born in County Durham into what he described as "cheerful poverty" in the year of the General Strike, the son of a trade union activist father who went on to became Mayor of South Shields. After graduating from Oxford and qualifying as a teacher, he sampled a number of careers before finding his true vocation as a writer. His first novel was published in 1957 and over 30 more followed under his own name and the pen-names James Munro and Patrick O'McGuire. His greatest success though, came as a writer for television. After contributing scripts to series such as The Avengers *and* The Troubleshooters, *he created the legendary anti-hero Callan in the television play* A Magnum for Schneider *and the character went on to feature in the eponymous television series (1967-72) and film, portrayed by Edward Woodward. Mitchell was credited with scriptwriting 30 episodes of the iconic television series, as well as five 'Callan' novels and a long-running series of short stories, first published in the* Sunday Express *between 1970 and 1976, many of which were syndicated to newspapers in Malaysia and Australia. James Mitchell went on to find even more success with the hit BBC drama series* When the Boat Comes In, *set in his native north-east.*

Mike Ripley is an award-winning crime writer and for ten years was the crime fiction critic of the Daily Telegraph. *He is currently writing a series of novels continuing the adventures of Margery Allingham's famous detective Albert Campion and is the Series Editor of the Ostara Crime imprint.*

Callan Uncovered 2

by

JAMES MITCHELL

Ostara Publishing

Ostara Publishing 2015

This collection © the Estate of James Mitchell, 2015

Stories and scripts © James Mitchell, 1967, 1969, 1970, 1971, 1972.

Hardback Edition   ISBN 9781909619241
Paperback Edition ISBN 9781909619234

A CIP reference is available from the British Library

Printed and Bound in the United Kingdom

Ostara Publishing
13 King Coel Road
Colchester
CO3 9AG
www.ostarapublishing.co.uk

Contents

Editor's Preface

Uncovering More Callan

The idea to try and collect together the Callan stories written by James Mitchell's for the *Sunday Express* in the early 1970s came about in 2013 when I was involved in editing new issues of three full-length Callan novels as Top Notch Thrillers.

Initial research on the internet suggested that there were nine or ten Callan stories, dedicated Callan fans put the number nearer 14. In the end, after several visits to the British Library, I found a total of 25. These were published, along with the script of an un-filmed *Callan* episode, as *Callan Uncovered* in 2014.

Even as the first rave reviews were going up on Amazon, one reader, Richard Savage, contacted me to ask why we had not included the ten stories he had cut from the *Sunday Express* in 1971 and 1972 and pasted into a Callan scrapbook. The reason we had not was quite simple: I was not – and neither were any of the knowledgeable *Callan* fans who had advised me – aware of their existence!

And so, following the lead given to me by Richard Savage, I returned to the British Library to consult their microfilm copies of the *Sunday Express* for 1971 and 1972. There indeed were the stories I had missed when compiling *Callan Uncovered*, but just to be sure I did what in spy fiction is known as "walking back the cat" and kept on going back through the archive. As a result, five more previously unreported stories, first published in September and October 1970, turned up!

It seems the Callan short stories began on 20th September 1970 when the *Sunday Express* announced:

CALLAN, the cynical, enigmatic agent in the rumpled raincoat, has won an enormous following among television viewers.

NOW Callan appears in a new medium – in a series of stories specially written for the Sunday Express by the author of the television series.

There followed the first story, *File on the Happy Hippy,* which opens *Callan Uncovered 2.* The 'Callan Casebook' as it became known soon secured a regular slot in the newspaper and when the 1971 series of stories was launched in August, *Express* readers were told: **Put a 'Do Not Disturb' notice by your deckchair. Callan will compel your undivided attention.**

Most of the stories conform to a similar structure and formula, but it was a formula James Mitchell had honed to perfection in his writing for television. The dialogue is tight and terse and descriptions of people and places are pared to the bone. In very few words, James Mitchell created a very complex character in David Callan, a character which had immediately struck a chord with the British public.

True, some of the stories are perhaps a little *too* formulaic and in some can be seen shades of television episodes, but Mitchell's skill was that, when least expected, we see Callan's vulnerability, even his compassion, and we get wonderfully sardonic reminders that Callan is fighting his own class war.

They are, of course, a product of their time, but the intervening 45 years have not been as unkind to them as might have been feared. True, political correctness these days would query some of the attitudes expressed towards women and to foreigners, but in the mainstream of popular culture of the time (and the *Sunday Express* itself), such expressions were of the minor and mild variety.

Politically, the stories pin their colours clearly to the mast and the mantra "better dead than Red" predominates. Again, allowances must be made for the era in which they were written. The Cold War was still pretty chilly, the Berlin Wall was intact (and seemed impregnable), the Soviet Union and the KGB were the go-to enemies of democracy and living standards in the West, although James Mitchell also recognised a clear and present danger from the HVA (*Hauptverwaltung Aufklüring*), the foreign espionage department of East Germany's notorious *Stasi*.

Most students, in the wake of the 1968 anti-Vietnam protests, were suspect, having been 'turned Red' or corrupted by drugs. Or both. But such were the attitudes at the time of writing.

All the stories here are reconstructed from copies taken from microfilms made almost twenty years ago from newspapers which were then at least twenty-five years old. It some cases, the quality of the microfilm and subsequent copies were not good and minor fragments of text were blurred or missing, requiring an editorial judgement call. Any mistakes made in repairing these (very small) cracks in the text, are my responsibility entirely.

In the year James Mitchell began to contribute short stories to the *Sunday Express* and the third series of *Callan* was broadcast on ITV, he compiled a 'file' on his enigmatic hero for the *TV Times*, which is reprinted here as **Get Callan** – an obvious reference to the (then) forthcoming film *Get Carter,* which along with *Callan* formed the twin pillars of British 'noir' fiction of the early 1970's.

Discounting the newspaper serialisation of the Callan novel *Russian Roulette* (which we republished in 2013 as a Top Notch Thriller), Ostara has now published the 40 known Callan short stories. I say 'known' as more may well come to light. That is why we have resisted the urge to use the expression 'The Complete Collection'. With Callan, you just never know...

Mike Ripley,
Colchester, June 2015.

Get Callan

To promote the third series of Callan *about to be broadcast on ITV, the* TV Times *carried extensive features on the cast, the show and its enigmatic 'anti-secret agent' hero David Callan. For Callan's background (and the 'story so far'), they turned to his 'controller', James Mitchell, to provide the following secret file which was published on 4ᵗʰ April 1970.*

From: Appointments Officer
To: Head of Sections
Subject: David Callan

Callan was born South London 1931 (Aged 38). Parents killed by V2 in 1944. Callan found their bodies on way home from school. From then lived with aunt until he joined the Army. Aunt now deceased.

Educated Junior School, Secondary Modern and Technical College. Left school 1946. Worked as apprentice to firm of locksmiths (attended technical courses on day release).

Army: Could have gone into Royal Engineers. Surprised employers by choosing Infantry (Green Howards). Highest possible ratings for initiative; unarmed combat; shooting. Very high survival factor. Promoted Corporal. Service in Malaya. His unit very successful in catching and killing Communist Chinese. Callan recommended for D.S.M. but involved in drunken brawl with Infantry Sergeants whom he beat up badly. Reduced to ranks. D.S.M. withheld. Demobbed 1952.

Resumed work at locksmiths. Suddenly and inexplicably attempted to rob jeweller's safe supplied by his firm. Caught by accident. Old night-watchman stumbled on to him, grabbed him and yelled. Callan, who could have killed him, didn't, and was caught. Sentenced to two years' imprisonment. Wormwood Scrubs. Released after 15 months. (Here he first met the burglar known as Lonely).

Hunter (I) took him into Section on basis of (a) Commando record; (b) burgling skill. Went to 'college' 1953-54. Developed skills in theft, unarmed combat and shooting. Dead-shot with pistol. First operation involved him in blackmail and killing. Very high rating.

From then until 1966 Callan carried out 19 missions, including 11 killings; 15 were complete success; two failed because of inadequate briefing; two because of failure of colleagues. Callan prefers to work alone. (This may influence attitude to colleagues).

By 1960 Callan was second-in-command to Hunter(I)who rated him very highly. Very possible next Head of Section. But in 1965 he killed a Russian spy whom he knew well and liked. From that time became too involved with the people who were his targets. Worked with the same skill, but increasing reluctance. Hunter tried to change him but failed.

Callan de-activated from Section in 1966. Trained as book-keeper, worked for wholesale grocer who believed him to be ex-convict.

Re-activated 1968. Complete success with Hunter(II) – AA rating in all operations. Complete success with Hunter(III) until brainwashed by KGB into killing him. Shortly afterwards, Callan was shot by Meres. After critical illness Callan is about to be discharged from hospital. Medically A1. No extensive psychiatric tests have yet been carried out.

Callan is a non-smoker, drinks Scotch, cautiously on a job, heavily on certain other occasions. Never drunk.

From: Hunter(IV)
To: Head of Sections
(No copies. Delivery and return by nominated messenger only)
Ref: DC/EO 17
Subject: Callan - Involvement with women
MOST SECRET

Remarkably little on file. I suspect this to be because Callan is an operative alert enough to conduct his amours when his colleagues aren't watching.

He appears to be quite adequately normal sexually. There can be no doubt of his attraction to women. There is a remarkable charm behind that brisk and witty ruthlessness. He has used it several times on Section business with success. He is, of course, also a risk to us, so far as women are concerned. That "capacity for involvement with other people" could, I am well aware, prove extremely embarrassing to himself and to my Section, but: (a) I am confident that I shall be aware of any danger from Callan in time to deal with it; (b) he himself has controlled the risk in the past, and I see no reason why he should not continue to do so, especially as

11

his control is motivated by the fear that the woman involved may be hurt by others - or by this Section.

Hunter (IV)

From: A.T.W.G. Snell
(Psychiatric Consultant to Section)
To: Head of Sections (Group)

Callan is a very healthy man with excellent reflexes, muscular co-ordination and eyesight. Physically he is again in good condition. There is no evidence at this stage to suggest that he has not fully recovered from brainwashing by KGB. However, tests in this area are incomplete and I consider this report to be an interim one.

I would add that since he has become aware of his responsibility for the death of Hunter(III) he has lost whatever little conception he had of the word "duty". The flaw - if one may so express it - already in his nature, i.e. his capacity for involvement with other people (consider his relationship with the petty criminal Lonely) has intensified and I would consider it even more likely to imperil a Section operation. For the record, Callan's I.Q. is still well above average. (Actual score withheld, as is usual in this Section). Rorschach and other tests show him to be of very stable mentality other than under the conditions stated. No evidence of inversion. Trend to sadism remains, but held in balance.

At this moment in time, despite his obvious abilities, I recommend Callan's withdrawal from the Section though finally, and no matter how irrelevantly, may I say this: I still like Callan.

A.T.W.G. Snell, MB, BCh, MRCP,DPS.

EXTRACT from transcribed tape recorder by D. T. Judd -
Armourer, Hunter's Section.
MOST SECRET

… So like I say the guy is good. Better than good. You know. Like great … Listen, when I was in the States I carried a gun for a mob in Youngstown, Ohio. They're tough there, believe me. The way most guys think they're tough. Know what I mean? Back there they chew walls and spit bricks - but I tell you - we never had one like Callan … The guy never misses. There's days I think he

12

can't miss. All he has to do is point - and bang! - you're dead … Brave? Don't ask me, Mister. Ask the guys he's killed. From what I hear they were mostly looking at him at the time … with guns in their hands …

From: Head of Sections
To: Hunter(IV)
(No copies. Delivery and return by nominated messenger only.)
Ref: DC/EO/17

Callan's background noted and acknowledged. Re-activation possible *provided* Snell is completely satisfied that he has passed the further psychiatric tests that Snell himself will devise. *If* Snell is *then* satisfied, Callan may be re-instated, in view of your failure to recruit sufficient operatives to handle Red File subjects, but in that event Callan must be very carefully controlled. What do you suggest?

Head of Sections

The Stories

First published in the *Sunday Express*:

File on the Happy Hippy

WHENEVER Hunter sent for you, you knew it was trouble, and when the secretary said: "Charlie asked me to tell you it was urgent," then you knew it was big trouble.

He looked at the photographs in the yellow file Hunter had given him. "Recognise her?" Hunter said. "Take your time." Long hair, a dress that looked vaguely Indian, hippy beads, bare feet. Pretty girl, with strong bones—and a strong will to match by the look of her.

Trouble all right—her kind usually were; for their parents. But big trouble? For Hunter?

This one must do something different. "I've never seen her, sir," Callan said.

"Her name is Cruze," said Hunter. "Janet Cruze. What I believe is called a hippy. She arrived in London last week. American citizen—and twenty-one two months ago. That's important."

He paused. "It's important because it means she's worth seven - and - a - half - million dollars."

"That should make her very happy," said Callan.

"It does indeed. But it distresses her father."

"He shouldn't have given it to her then."

"He didn't," said Hunter. "It's her mother's money. When she died she left it all to the daughter. I doubt if Cruze himself is worth two million."

"Poor chap," said Callan. "How does he manage?"

"Cruze is a career diplomat," Hunter said. "A good one. He may well be the next U.S. Ambassador to Great Britain—and soon. Our masters consider that this would be an excellent thing. He is. I gather, very well disposed to us. The girl is, of course, his weakness. If there were to be a scandal now...."

"Is it likely?"

"Extremely. The CIA seem to think that the opposition has already reached her."

"KGB?"

"Possibly. It could be the Poles or the East Germans. Whoever it is, they'll try to persuade her to do something foolish. Your job is to prevent them."

Trouble all right. The biggest.

Callan went to his flat, made one phone call, packed a bag, then took a taxi to a Chelsea mews, as Hunter had ordered. Nice. Trees in the yards, shrubs in pots, window-boxes, and one broken blossom waiting by his door.

"I got your message, Mr Callan," Lonely said.

"I see you did," said Callan, and took out a key, opened the front door. Lonely's hand came down on his.

"Mr Callan," he said, "we're not breaking and entering are we? Not in daylight."

Callan turned away and said. "Will you for Gawd's sake get down-wind?"

"I don't like daylight jobs," said Lonely.

"We're not doing a job," said Callan. "This place belongs to a friend of mine. He's lending it to me for a few days."

"But what do you want me for, Mr Callan?" Lonely asked.

"There's a bird coming to see me," Callan said. "When she does—I want you to follow her—if she's alone. If she isn't I want you to follow whoever comes with her. Twenty-five a day and food. All right?"

"Smashing," said Lonely.

"Make us a cup of tea, then," Callan said.

She didn't show for two days, and when she did, they watched her from behind the curtain as the Bentley that had brought her sealed off the mews.

"She's one of them hippies," said Lonely.

"What do you care?"

"Some of them don't take baths," said Lonely. "Some don't even bother to wash."

"Oh, mate," said Callan, but the little man meant it, and went on to hide himself, grumbling.

"I'm Janet Cruze," she said "Juby Geary said I should look you up."

"Fine," said Callan, and stood aside. As she passed him he looked out. Geezer waiting in the Bentley. At least it looked like a geezer; with these ruddy hippies you could never be sure. Another problem for Lonely....

She was looking around the sitting-room, a shrewd and assessing look that said *This doesn't look like a pusher's pad.*

"Have you known Juby long?" she asked.

"Since he flunked out of Princeton and went to live in Halght-Ashbury." Callan said, just like it was written in his instructions. "He used to come to me for pot."

"Boy, you sure get down to business," the girl said.

"Isn't that why you're here?"

"What makes you think that?"

"You mentioned Juby Geary," Callan said. "They only do that when they want a smoke."

She flushed then, an angry, unbecoming scarlet.

"You don't go much on a sales-pitch, do you?" she said.

"Why should I?" said Callan. "You want the stuff."

"I want a hundred smokes," she said.

16

"A hundred?"

"For cash," she said. "United States currency."

"You don't smoke it here," he said.

"I don't smoke it—period," said the girl. "Surprised?"

He made no answer. "I have friends who do," she said, and looked at the decanters on his drinks table, "but they don't drink Scotch. What are you anyway? A crook?"

"You know," said Callan. "I'd always heard you flower children were gentle and sensitive."

"I like to know who I'm dealing with."

"If your friend want to smoke," said Callan, "you're dealing with me."

Before she could rise to that there was a knock at the door. Callan opened it to a wild man: stained jeans, psychedelic shirt, bare feet, a three-week growth of unsuccessful beard. Looks as if this one drugs, Callan thought, but his body isn't beaten—not yet. Early twenties, chunky and fast. He tried to push past Callan, and found he couldn't, then stumbled and grabbed at his arms for support.

"Janet's here," he said.

Behind Callan. Janet spoke.

"I'm always here. Danny boy." To Callan she said, "Let him in."

"What's he on?" Callan said. "Heroin, morphine?"

"I take a little acid," Danny boy said. "Where's the harm?"

"No harm at all," said Callan. "Go and take it somewhere else."

Janet Cruze sighed. "Go wait in the car, Danny," she said.

When he stumbled off, she said, "You're not exactly polished yourself."

"This is where I live," said Callan. "Some kinds of dirt I won't let in here."

She left him then, and Callan heard the Bentley's whisper of power followed by the slow putt-putt of Lonely's hired scooter.

He picked up the phone and dialled the number, made his report.

"Nice," said Hunter. "Really nice. She'll be back I think—if only to dislike you all over again. Besides, that marijuana was something rather special. ... Did you say something?"

"I said 'I hate my job,'" said Callan. "But I said it to myself."

"So long as you don't say it to me. ... This Danny—he really drugs?"

"It looks like it."

"And yet you believe he—er—frisked you?"

"I know he did," said Callan. "But I wasn't carrying a gun."

"Perhaps you should," said Hunter. "Keep in touch."

Lonely was gone an hour, and came back to tell of wonders. "The bird took the geezer to a place up Notting Hill way and dropped him, then she came back to the Dorchester and I went back to Notting Hill. Weird place it was, Mr Callan. Big house, full of hippies. Must have been twelve to a room. What they call a common."

Callan thought for a moment. "A commune," he said.

"One of them invited me in."

"Did you go?"

"Course not," said Lonely. "Filthy dirty it was. But there's a phone booth over the road. Watched from there for a bit. Funny."

"What?"

"The bird's geezer. He was at a window—I could have sworn he was watching me—then the next thing I knew he was acting like a lunatic trying to jump out. It took six of them to hold him back."

"I hope he wasn't on to you," said Callan.

"Me an' all," said Lonely. "He's a nutter."

She came back three times, to buy more grass, and always her arrogance sparked against his. Each time she came alone.

She was alone too when the taxi brought her to him at one in the morning. She was high as a kite, and the cabby in terror that a copper might see her. Callan yanked her out of the cab, and went inside for money. When he came back the cab was gone, and Janet lay sprawled against the wall.

"I gave him something," she said. "I guess it must have been enough."

Callan carried her inside: The sweet-sour fumes of marijuana still clung to her.

"To what do I owe the pleasure?" he said.

"I've been to the commune," said Janet. "I couldn't go back to the Dorchester like this, could I?"

"So naturally you thought of me?"

"Naturally," she said. "After all, you sold me the stuff."

"You said you didn't use it."

"Danny said it was time I did."

"And you always do what Danny says?"

"I owe Danny," she said, "I owe him."

"For what?"

"The acid," she said. "I got him on the acid."

And it all came out, all the buried things the drug made it so easy to disinter.

She and her father had quarrelled over the Student Power friends she'd made at college, and she'd drifted from one hippy group to another, each one more outrageous than the last, till she'd met Danny—diffident, nervous, anxious to join, and the group she was with had initiated him with LSD for which she had paid—and after that he was hooked—and she was responsible: she the observer, never the participant. Until tonight. She had made him what he was.

"Why did he make you smoke?" Callan asked.

She shrugged. "Revenge, I guess. I had it coming."

"Do you love him?"

"Oh, brother," she said. "What you don't know about love." She lay back, her eyelids drooped. In seconds she was asleep.

Callan went to the phone, and Hunter said. "I'll ask. ... Hold on." After two minutes he was back. "Half of Fleet Street's at the Dorchester," he said. "Tip-off about a junky millionairess. You've done well, David."

"I haven't finished yet," said Callan, and hung up. When he went back Janet was writhing in nightmare. He took her in his arms and the writhing eased.

18

When Danny came to the mews Callan was alone. A brisk woman from the American Embassy had picked Janet up and promised her that everything would be fine—just fine. But Danny didn't know that. He came through Callan's window deft and easy, and made for the bedroom. Callan spoke from behind the kitchen door.

"She's gone," he said. "You can't reach her now."

Danny froze, and the lights came on. He wore the same clothes as always, plus a battered combat jacket.

"Turn round," said Callan. "Slowly," and Danny did so.

"Who are you?" Callan asked. "KGB?"

"I don't dig you, man," said Danny.

"You dig all right," said Callan. "That LSD stuff's a fake. Nobody takes trips alone."

"I think you're a fake too," Danny said, "a fake from the Section."

Callan observed that the hippy accent had gone completely, and that behind the beard and dropout clothes there was a very hard man indeed.

"That's right," he said.

"But you're wrong about one thing," said Danny. "You and I—*we* take trips alone. In our business we have to."

His right hand flashed for the gun beneath the coat.

Callan fired first.

File on a Faithful Husband

"HIS NAME'S Dekker," Hunter said. "Albrecht Dekker. Came to us in sixty-seven—from Munich. We cleared him and loaned him to the West Germans. He was good. They used him a lot. So did I."

Callan looked at the photograph. Dekker looked good—no question of it. The face was a clever one—and strong.

"The only trouble was he tricked me," Hunter said. "That doesn't seem possible, does it?"

"He was a plant?" Callan asked.

"He worked double right from the beginning. Betrayed five West German agents—and two of ours. Got out in time, too. Came to London to see me—got the tip he was blown—and vanished."

"You want me to find him?" Callan asked.

"No," said Hunter. "That's been done already."

He leaned forward took the photograph from Callan, and put it back in its file inevitably, the file's colour was red.

"I want you to kill him," said Hunter.

Dekker was in the Montcalm Hotel, a grim little Bastille in Bloomsbury that might have been made for him. Almost its entire clientele was middle-aged, male, sedentary, and foreign: research workers at the British Museum, delegates to minor conferences, salesmen suffering from a lack of faith in their products—Dekker could have been any of these.

Callan watched him in the restaurant, eating a revolting shepherd's pie with a thoroughness that could only be Teutonic. But then half the men in the dining-room *were* Teutons.

Bigger than I thought he would be, Callan thought. He can look after himself that one. But why should he? Why doesn't he go to an embassy? The Russians could get him out fast enough. Or the Czechs. Or the Poles.

But if he did that, we'd pick him up on his way there because the embassies are the first places we'd watch and he knows this. Hunter would call me and I'd take him anyway. ... No not *"take,"* he told himself. The word is *"kill,"* old son. You're a killer.

He pushed his plate away.

"Can I get you anything else, sir?" the waitress asked.

"You're joking," said Callan. Then—"All right. Coffee."

He spun the coffee out till Dekker got up to leave, and at once the two men behind him got up too. Younger than the average, these two, walking behind Dekker, shielding him. One of them held a cigarette in his left hand, but he reached for the door right-handed.

Callan went out to a public phone, dialled the long, unlisted number.

"Let me speak to Charlie, please," he said, and was put through at once.

"He's got two bodyguards," said Callan.

Hunter said: "You're sure?"

"I'm sure," said Callan. "They walk right, position right, and they keep their right hands free. If you want to set up an accident—it won't be easy."

"I don't want an accident," said Hunter. "I want him shot."

'It'll be World War Three," said Callan.

"It must be known that he has been executed," said Hunter. "The West Germans are insisting on it. You'll have to work out a story, of course."

Callan said: "I'll need help."

"You shall have it," Hunter said.

"Tell me something," Callan said. "Why doesn't he just fly out now?"

"He's waiting for his wife, I think." said Hunter. "He is a remarkably uxorious man. A mistake in our business, don't you think?"

Then he hung up before Callan could ask what uxorious meant.

Next day he bought a pocket dictionary that told him uxorious meant "excessively fond of one's wife." Callan got a receipt for it, and marked the cost down on his expense sheet, then he settled down to work out a plan.

It couldn't be the hotel. Too many people, too many telephones, Panda cars all over the place. Lift him from his minders, plant him somewhere quiet—then—do it. Lifting him would be the hardest thing of all—until the moment came when he would have to point the gun like an accusing finger, and squeeze the trigger. Leave that. Callan thought. Just leave it. Concentrate on getting rid of the heavies....

He looked down at the dictionary. Its pages had flipped back. *"Underworld,"* he read. *"The abode of the dead."* But that wasn't quite right, was it? They weren't all dead that lived there...

"You want me to break into Room 352 Mr Callan?" Lonely said.

"That's right."

"Then I lift whatever looks good?"

"Right."

"Then I plant it in Room 235?"

"Right again. How many more times?"

"Mr Callan—I don't get it," Lonely said.

"All you get is a hundred quid if you do the job—and a belting, if you don't."

"Ah well," said Lonely, "if you put it that way."

"I do," said Callan.

"Well in that case you're on," said Lonely. "But I still don't get it."

21

It worked very nicely—all the pieces meshed. The two heavies shared a double room, 235, and took it in turns to use the spare bed. Dekker had a double to himself, 237.

Lonely did the job while they dined at seven-forty-five. By eight o'clock he had phoned Callan—and Callan rang the number that Hunter had given him. The police arrived inside three minutes, almost, thought Callan, as if they'd been waiting round the corner, and grinned.

Up to 235, check the stuff there: two transistor tape recorders, three transistor radios Swiss-made, all good stuff, and a travelling wallet with a Swiss Air Ticket, Swiss passport, seven pounds in ones and 1,300 Swiss francs in travellers cheques. Not bad for 15 minutes.

Then back to the dining-room and pick them up fast, before the gun-hands could move. Six coppers, two heavies. They hadn't a chance, not against that six—and they knew it. Funny, though, that it took six of them to collar two tea-leaves, and all six of them armed, and one of them German speaking.

The dining-room was fluttering like a hen-roost that's just heard a fox. The loudest of the lot was a Swiss rep, the occupant of Room 352 who didn't even know he'd been robbed yet, and became a devotee of Scotland Yard the instant he did. But Dekker wasn't fluttering. As Hunter had said, he was good.

He walked straight out of the dining-room, out of the hotel, and called a cruising cab. It pulled up at once, and Dekker got in, then hesitated. There was a man in the passenger seat.

"I'm sorry," said Dekker.

"You should be," said Callan. "Get in."

Dekker looked into the barrel of the Magnum 38. He had never seen a more convincing argument.

"Take the jump seat," said Callan, and Dekker obeyed. The cab moved off at once.

"You're making a terrible mistake," said Dekker.

"Not this time," Callan said. "Five West German agents we could learn to live with—but two of ours. You got greedy, Dekker."

Dekker signed.

"How will you kill me?" he asked.

"With this," said Callan.

"You will shoot me here?"

"No," said Callan. "Not here. ... You bought a girl for the night. She took you to a place where you could have a little fun—only your idea of fun wasn't hers. You belted her a bit too hard and she yelled—and her minder came in.

"You belted him too, so the minder shot you. Then they scarpered. ... Nobody else saw them or heard them—they never do in the place we're going to—but that's how the coppers will reconstruct the crime."

Dekker said: "You cannot do this."

"Believe me, mate," said Callan. "Believe me."

"You cannot make me die like that," said Dekker. "I have never been with a prostitute. Never."

"You had seven men killed," said Callan. "It's a bit late to be squeamish."

Dekker made a grab for him, and Callan belted him with the gun-barrel, easing the force of the blow so that Dekker was stunned only, and fell back against the partition. The cab driver didn't even look back.

When Dekker recovered he was weeping.

"Please," Dekker said. *"Please."*

Callan was silent.

"I have to die," said Dekker. "I accept that. I think we all do—"

'Belt up," said Callan.

"Please hear me," Dekker said. "I must not die this way."

He struggled for the calm that would give him the words he needed in the other man's language.

"My wife," he said. *"I love my wife. You cannot know how much I love her. Please do not let it be this way."*

The taxi stopped.

"Out," said Callan.

Dekker first, then Callan behind him and to one side, as if he were a bodyguard.

A house once elegant, and now decayed, rooms to let by the day, the night, the hour, and the doors of those rooms tightly shut. Nobody nosey, nobody calling coopers, no matter what you did.

"This one," said Callan, and Dekker went inside.

A tumbled bed, a torn pair of tights, an overturned bottle of gin, a riding crop with a ribbon of baby-blue silk tied to its base.

Dekker moved faster than Callan believed a human being could move, one hand grabbing for the gun, the other clawing for his throat.

Callan brought his knee up and Dekker's hands grew weak, but he hung on till the gun-barrel swing again and his head crashed into the mantel-shelf, the grimy elegant mantel-shelf of sharp-edged marble.

There was no need to squeeze the trigger. Callan looked down at the dead man and marveled.

Aloud he said, *"So that's what uxorious means."*

He put the gun away, pressed Dekker's fingerprints to the gin bottle, the glass and the whip. Hunter wouldn't exactly go mad with love over this one. Hunter wanted Dekker shot, and all Callan had given him was a belting. Well, Hunter could lump it. A pimp would have used a cosh anyway.

File on a Loving Sister

HUNTER had said: "They all seem to think that Matthews will go to a safe house." And Callan had thought so too.

After all, a man who had stolen defence agreement files from the Far East desk of the Foreign Office and flogged them to Chairman Mao for an estimated fifty thousand quid, and cheap at the price—you'd think even the Chinks would find a safe house for him. But Hunter wouldn't have it.

"Not Matthews," he'd said. "Matthews isn't an idealist—he's a money-grubber. A thief. And thieves don't trust anybody—unless they have to."

Callan had said: "That's right," because he knew all about thieving, and Hunter knew it.

"If they have to," Hunter had said, "they trust somebody who loves them. To be loved is a very powerful weapon, Callan. Thieves like that … I think you should become a friend of Matthews's sister."

That had been six weeks ago, and Matthews was still missing, and Callan was his sister's friend. Enid Matthews. Aged 33. Shy, very shy. Could have been pretty if she'd had the nerve — only she hadn't. Cover-up clothes and a hairstyle that did nothing for her except keep the hair out of her eyes. A teacher. Secondary Modern—out in some dump in the suburbs where they went to bed before the pubs shut. Fond of literature. So Callan had joined the literary society, and tried not to yawn when people could see him.

The trouble was, she was nice. He'd had to work at it, but his brand of diffidence and gentleness appealed to her, made her feel safe. Then he could talk intelligently too—and read, despite the fact that he'd left school at 15. That helped. The schoolteacher in her ached to show him how to use what he had.

Six weeks ago that had been and no mention of her brother. They all knew who she was, of course, but nobody told him. They respected her: all the literary society crowd. She was—nice. He'd told Hunter there was nothing doing, but Hunter had said he'd to hold on anyway. There'd be a break soon. He had no doubt that Matthews was still in the country—and frantic to get out. Only see if you can speed it up a bit, David old chap.

Speed it up. Make her trust you. Show her you're somebody she can use. All she knew so far was that he was a clerk—out of work but with a bit put by—come back to the neighbourhood to look after his

24

ailing mum. Nice and safe and dependable. But how could she use him?

He took her to the pictures, and she let him pay, but afterwards she bought the supper because he was out of a job. Then they walked back to her house, and she was close to him, and for the first time not bothered by it. Not bothered at all.

When he kissed her she went rigid, at first, but his hands were gentle and patient, and she yielded at last—yielded and clung, and he could sense how frightened she was, how desperate, beneath the prim schoolteacher facade.

He said at last. "I think I'm falling in love with you." The street lamp showed him the joy in her face, the sense of power the word always gave: and then something else. A kind of truth, a decency.

She said: "I don't think you know much about me."

"It's mutual," said Callan.

"No," she said, "It's not. I'm—Frank Matthews's sister."

His face showed only bewilderment.

"The spy," she said. "The man who sold all those secrets to the Chinese."

"I didn't know anything about that," he said. "I—I've been away for a bit. And anyway—it's not your brother I'm talking about."

"You don't mind?" She seemed amazed; even—or so it seemed to him—disappointed. But when he kissed her the disappointment fled.

He heard plenty about Frank after that. How brilliant he'd been at school and won a scholarship to Cambridge and passed the Foreign Office exam. How he'd adored his mother, who'd died when he was sixteen, and Enid had had to bring him up because he'd never seen his father, killed in the Normandy landings—half a lifetime ago.

A good boy, she said. A gentle boy. A boy who'd never hurt anybody. And Callan thought—*she means it.* Even now she means it, even though he's sold secrets that could cost thousands of lives. Because he's easily led, you see. Got in with a rich crowd and wanted to look as good as they were. That's how it happened.

He told her that he understood, and that he loved her, and she was happy. And with the happiness she was pretty. Her eyes sparkled, her lips parted: suddenly she really was a woman to be loved.

Lonely was frankly bewildered, and said so.

"You don't want me to thieve nothing, Mr Callan?" he asked.

"Not this time."

"Just talk? About when we done bird together?"

"That's right," Callan said. "Tell her about how nice I was."

"Well, you was nice," said Lonely. "You were a good friend to me."

Callan said quickly. "There's a tenner in it for you."

Inside, he could feel nothing at all, except disgust at himself.

"This one's on the house," said Lonely. "All I have to do is tell the truth, Mr Callan."

Callan said: "Don't call me Mr Callan. Call me Dave."

"Just as you say, Mr Callan," said Lonely.

But it was all right on the night—after a lot of rehearsal. He took her to a pub and Lonely came in, and inside three minutes she knew he'd done bird Lonely came over all coy and embarrassed, and had to be bought a drink. Several drinks. And each time Callan went to the bar to get them, he told her what a good mate Dave Callan had been. A hard geezer, sure—but one that looked out for his friends.

Once he went up to help Callan, and said: "You got a real lady there. Mr Callan."

Callan said: "Keep calling me Dave."

Lonely left at last, and the two of them walked back to her house. At the door he made no attempt to touch her. "So now you know," said Callan. "Goodbye. You won't see me again. But I meant what I said."

"No. wait," she said. "Come inside. Please, I want you to."

They went inside to her sitting-room. She came into his arms and they kissed. *Courting*, Callan thought. *Courting in the parlour.* Hunter would laugh if he knew. But Callan wasn't laughing. This girl *needed* love. She had given for too long.

They sat hand in hand and whispered where no one could overhear them. About each other and, at last, about how happy they would be— once Frank was safe.

Cautiously, reluctantly, Callan said. "I could get him out."

"Oh, David, could you?" she said.

He said, "I'd thought I was finished with all this." His voice was bitter.

"You will be," she said. "I promise. But please—we've got to help Frank."

It was strange, he thought, how easily the weak ones could tie the strong ones down.

"It'll cost you," he said.

"How much?"

He shrugged. "Depends on the contract. About a grand." He saw her puzzlement. "A thousand quid," he said. "You've got a lot to learn." The bitterness was still in his voice.

"Please. David," she said. "Forgive me. He was all I had—till you."

"I won't take anything," he said, and she came back to his arms.

She made contact with Frank, but it took her four days to persuade him that it was safe—and then at last he broke cover. Dead lucky, he'd been. A fishing holiday in the Wye Valley—and nobody had even wondered. All Callan had to do was hire him a car, pick him up, and drive him over to Kent, he told her, where the contact would be waiting.

She insisted on going with him, and he dared not refuse her. It would make her suspicious. It was a lovely day and she was happy, the valley of the Wye enchanted her.

Her brother was at the hotel—brand new luggage, expensive trout rod. Bronzed and fit, thought Callan, and as weak as water. It was Callan who put the luggage in the boot—and Callan who drove, while Matthews sat in the back with his sister, whining about the thousand pounds.

The pick-up wasn't supposed to happen till Oxford, but they grabbed him just outside Cheltenham. It was neatly done. Nice quiet road, two cars coming up quick, then him jammed between them, stopping when they did. Four men a from Special Branch, and Hunter had come along too, to make sure all was well.

One of the Special Branch men made the speech: "Frank Matthews I arrest you—" and Enid clung to him and wept, and didn't see Callan at all.

Hunter said, "You handled this one nicely, David."

Callan said, "But you didn't trust me. You said you'd make the collar at Oxford."

"When you started this one I told you that to be loved is a very powerful weapon," said Hunter. "It applies to you too, you know." He looked at the girl. "Do you want to take her in?"

"No," said Callan. "Let one of them do it. I'll ride with you."

As he opened the door, Enid faced him at last. Her prettiness had gone, and it was hard to believe it would ever return. Her face held only vulnerability now, and bewilderment.

"I don't understand," she said. "You said you loved me."

"I meant it," said Callan.

File on a Painless Dentist

"A DENTIST?" said Callan. Hunter nodded.

"From what I can gather a very good dentist," he said. "Calls himself Clarkson. Here."

He pushed over the red file, and Callan looked at the face. This geezer even looked like a dentist. There was a combination of force and blandness about him: the sort of calm strength that belongs only with those who pull teeth.

"After all," said Hunter, "it's not a bad way to run a clearing house. People are in and out of a dentist's surgery all the time. If his agents care to drop in to make a report they can have a filling done free."

"What's his real name?" Callan asked.

"We rather fancy it's Orlov," Hunter said. "We'd like you to make sure. As you know we don't possess a photograph of Orlov himself." Callan looked again at the bland, strong face.

"Patterson, Chalmers, and Gregg," he said. "Orlov got them all, didn't he?"

"Yes," said Hunter. "But then he's extremely able. We've always known that. I hope you're aware of it too, Callan."

"If it is Orlov—you want me to kill him?"

"I do indeed—if it is Orlov. Otherwise bring him in for interrogation."

"How long do I have to find out?"

"Unfortunately there isn't a great deal of time. He's expecting a man down from Holy Loch next week—a chap with information about American submarines. It would be as well if he were dead before this chap came to see him." He looked at Callan. "We intercepted a signal. He's being recalled once the Holy Loch man leaves."

Callan said: "I don't like rush jobs."

"My dear boy, who does?" said Hunter. "How are your teeth by the by?"

"The ones I've got left are fine."

Clarkson lived out in Kent, nice and handy for the Channel ports, and a 20-minute drive from a fast road that would whip him up to London and Heathrow airport inside the hour. He had a nice practice in a quiet square; solid, Georgian houses at twenty thousand a-piece. He'd been there for years and everybody liked him. Big noise in Rotary, paid his whack to all the local charities, five handicap at golf. And absolutely painless, everybody said. Couldn't stand the thought of hurting you. And everybody believed it: but Callan knew that Gregg had taken three days to die, and that death had come in the middle of a scream.

He liked women too, according to his receptionist. Callan met her in one of those terrible English tea-rooms that somehow still, survive in country towns, all plastic chintz and poached eggs on toast and yesterday's tea. She'd had something going with Clarkson herself, once upon a time. Callan thought, and she still fancies him a bit. Now let's see if she can fancy me.

It wasn't all that difficult. Well past thirty, with the first signs of desperation. Birds like that were meat and drink to the kind of travelling rep Callan pretended to be. She never even found time to ask him what he was selling. Just went on and on about Clarkson, the reception-room, even the surgery. Too much chat: far too much, but most of that was nerves, and anyway. Callan was a good listener, and her flat was comfortable.

He went back to London to see Lonely. There was no point in telephoning him, not about a dentist. The little man was almost as terrified of dentists as he was of Callan. Ask him nicely, that was the way, and only get rough if he had to. So he took him to a cowboy picture and bought him beer and fish and chips, and then more beer.

It was over the fish and chips that Lonely got suspicious. "How did you know I was broke, Mr Callan?" he asked.

"I guessed," said Callan, and passed him the vinegar.

"Well I must say it's very I kind of you. Very kind indeed. Only..."

"Only what?"

"Is there something you want?"

"No," said Callan. "Just thought you might fancy a treat, that's all."

"Oh I do, Mr Callan."

"There is one small thing," Callan said. "Mind you, I wouldn't ask you to do it for nothing...."

"No punch-ups," said Lonely. "I'm sorry, Mr Callan, but..."

"Who said anything about punch-ups?"

"All this beer and fish and chips," said Lonely simply. "And stall seats. And iced lollies."

"Lonely, old son," Callan said. "I wouldn't get you mixed up in violence. You haven't got the build for it."

"I know, Mr Callan, but..."

"Belt up," said Callan, still keeping it friendly. "I'm going to tell you how to make a hundred quid."

For a while it was easy, until he told Lonely that Clarkson was a dentist, and after that he stank worse than the fish and chips.

"Mr Callan, I daren't," he said. "Not a dentist. You should just see what that one in the Scrubs did to me."

He opened his mouth, but Callan gripped his chin, pushed his face away, the fingers, gentle at first, squeezing to the edge of pain.

"I was next to you," said Callan, "I know. But you're doing it." The fingers squeezed harder. "Well?"

"Whatever you say, Mr Callan."

"You better mean that, son."

When he left the little man, he put in a call to Charlie, and Hunter came on at once.

"Are you sure it's Orlov?" Hunter asked.

"Almost," said Callan.

"I want you absolutely sure. And in the next two days. After that it's too late."

"It'll be tomorrow," said Callan, and began to explain. Hunter heard him out in silence, then said: "I don't like you going in alone."

"Two of us would never get near," said Callan. "He knows I'm alone."

"Yes, out even so...." He paused. Callan was right. "Like you, I hate rush jobs," he said. "Your plan is acceptable. But remember this—Clarkson is very good indeed."

"Sometimes I think I am too," said Callan. "Now I'm going to find out."

Next day he was by the bus stop when Lonely arrived. (Never do to let Lonely come up by train; this was commuter country.) But put him on a bus and Lonely was just about invisible. He followed you that way too, about as noisy as a leaf in a gutter.

They reached the Georgian square a little ahead of time, and Callan took a walk round the square while he waited, and thought: *This is the most natural thing in the world - a bloke putting off a visit to the dentist* and noticed, without surprise, that his knees were shaking.

He looked round the square to find that Lonely had vanished, then stepped into a phone booth, flicked over the pages until he saw the receptionist leave Clarkson's house with the happy urgency that says as plain as words that the day's work is over.

"I'm sorry, darling," Callan said to himself, "but if I get lucky you're out of a job." He watched her out of sight, then walked slowly across to the dentist's, pressed the bell to make muted chimes. It was a minute before the door opened, and Callan wiped his hands on his handkerchief. Nothing wrong with that, either. Not outside a dentist's. Then the door opened and Clarkson stood there, heavy shoulders straining a white smock, A. J. Clarkson B.D.S. (Lond.), alias Piotr Orlov, K.G.B.

"I'm sorry," he said. "My surgery is closed."

"Please," said Callan. "If you don't mind. I'm in a lot of pain."

At the word "pain," Orlov's expression changed. If you didn't know you would have thought he was feeling compassion.

"Come in," said Orlov. "I'll see what I can do."

Down a hall, white-painted, pastel carpet, into a waiting-room dominated by a vast bookcase, then on to the surgery: stainless steel sink, the huge and always terrifying chair, lamps curled away like snakes. The risk he was about to take terrified Callan, but there was no other way.

"Sit in the chair, please. Let me take a look." Reluctantly—at the dentist's you're always reluctant – Callan obeyed.

Lonely, old son, let's hope you've got it right.

"Now then," said Orlov, "let's see where this nasty pain is. Open wide."

Callan obeyed and pointed with one finger. Orlov used a probe and Callan winced and yelled.

"Odd," said Orlov. "I can't see anything."

He pulled down a lamp and pressed the switch. Callan closed his eyes just in time. The light burned on his eyelids and he felt a sudden relaxation of the pressure on his left shoulder. When he opened his eyes, squinting against the light, he saw that Orlov held his gun.

"You told my receptionist your name is Peters." Callan stayed silent. "You told her you were a sales representative." He lifted the gun. "You have unconventional methods of selling."

"Did she tell you that?" Callan asked.

"No," said Orlov. "She isn't involved. I bugged her flat some time ago."

Callan thought: *I know you did, you bastard. I saw the bugs.*

Orlov smiled. "Security, you know. And you do know, don't you?" Callan said nothing. "Tell me, Mr...Peters, which firm do you represent – Patterson, Chalmers and Gregg?" Again, no answer.

Orlov picked up a drill left-handed.

"You have rather a lot to tell me," he said, the gun aimed suddenly at Callan's belly. "Lie back, shut your eyes and open your mouth," said Orlov and Callan obeyed.

Lonely, old son, come on.

"I'm afraid this is going to hurt a great deal," Orlov said.

Through slitted lids Callan saw him take two steps – and then it happened. Lonely pulled the bookcase in the waiting-room over, exactly as Callan had told him to do. Callan was braced for it, but it shook him even so and Orlov spun towards the sound knowing as he did so that he had made the ultimate mistake. Callan came out of the chair like a missile.

Lonely was waiting for Callan in his car. The little man was shaking. "I told you to wait beside it," said Callan. "How did you get in? I thought I left it locked."

"You never lose the knack once you've learned it," Lonely said. "And, anyway, I got scared. Blimey, that noise."

Callan started the motor, eased the car into the street. After ten miles the little man relaxed. "Seems a bit daft to me, breaking into a geezer's home just to pull his bookcase over, just because he switches a light on," Lonely said.

"Look in the glove compartment," said Callan.

Lonely looked, found a wad of notes and counted happily. "Just right, Mr Callan. Ta," he said. He leaned back. "Funny," he said.

"What's funny?"

"Well, you know me and dentists. I was out of his house that fast— but I thought I heard another bang. Sort of like a shot."

"Don't talk daft," said Callan. "Who ever heard of a dentist being drilled?"

File on a Fancy Lawyer

"HIS NAME'S Davenport," said Hunter. "Christopher Mainwaring Davenport."

Callan looked at the photograph. Good looks running a little to flesh. Savile Row suit, club tie. "He looks like it," he said.

"What d'you make of him?"

Callan hesitated. "Company director?"

"Among other things. He is also a lawyer, Crimmond, Davenport & Fee. Offices in the Temple. All that sort of thing. Very successful lawyers."

"That's why he's in a yellow file?"

"No. I want him watched because he's too successful. His taxable income is of the order of fifteen thousand a year—but he lives at rather more than three times that rate."

"Fiddling the books? That's a rozzer's job."

"As a lawyer he's a model of probity," said Hunter.

"If that means he's honest he must back horses."

"Only those he owns," Hunter paused. "He gets about quite a bit. Newmarket, Ascot, ambassadorial parties, first nights."

"Not exactly my scene, is it?" Callan said.

"As a barman you might have possibilities," said Hunter. "Explore them. Find out why Davenport has so much money."

Barman wasn't on. Too static, and Davenport moved about all the time. Nice places too. The Savoy Grill, cocktail bar at the Hilton, theatres, discotheques. And embassies. All sorts of embassies. What we need, thought Callan, is transport....

Lonely said, "Mr Callan I daren't. Not without a licence."

"I got you a licence," said Callan, and handed it over.

"But I haven't driven a cab in years," said Lonely.

"It's like riding a bike. Once you've done it, you never lose the knack—and it pays you fifty a day on top of what you make."

They put in three days of *dolce vita*. If Davenport didn't know anything else, he knew all about enjoying himself. Wherever he appeared corks popped and champagne flowed, and money flowed too, at gaming clubs, race-courses, bridge games. Callan and Lonely used a cab apiece and followed him everywhere. All Davenport seemed to do was have a good time. Lonely was exhausted just watching.

On the fourth day Callan rang in and made his report.

"You sound tired," said Hunter.

Callan said. "I'm whacked. When does this geezer sleep?"

"And you've discovered nothing?"

"Not a thing. He's met a lot of people and he's had a lot of fun—but he hasn't *done* anything."

"He went to three embassies."

"Him and about a thousand other people. They were embassy parties. French Embassy on Monday, yesterday was—."

"No names," said Hunter.

Sitting in his own office, phone with the scrambler on, and he said no names. That made it the most secret job of all.

"You know where he went last night?" Hunter said.

"I followed him," said Callan.

"We had a man at that party—watching Davenport. He saw him talking to the cultural attaché for twenty minutes. You know who the cultural attaché is?"

"Their top agent," said Callan. "How did Davenport look?"

"Greedy," said Hunter. "Stay with him."

Next day was morning at the office, lunch at the Connaught, afternoon in court, cocktails at the Savoy, first night followed by supper at the Caprice. He talked to two girls who looked like models, a major in the Coldstreams, two barristers, five actors, and a judge. The day was typical. Davenport worked, spent money, nattered with top people. He didn't do a bloody thing.

Next day Callan observed Davenport lunching at a pub: the lager and sandwich lunch that gets sold by the hundreds of thousands every working day: Next to him was a thin, sad geezer with a beer and a sandwich and a copy of that day's Standard. He and Davenport didn't look at each other, didn't speak, but when you'd been in the game as long as Callan had, you knew. The thin, sad geezer was going to make a live drop, and Davenport was the collector.

Callan watched from behind a small Scotch and water, and sure enough the thin, sad one put his Standard down on the bar and went to a table to eat his sandwich. At once Davenport picked up the Standard, glanced at it, stuck it in his pocket. He didn't unfold it. To Callan's eye it looked bulkier than that day's edition should have been.

Then Davenport went over to the thin, sad geezer and handed him an envelope. "I think you dropped this," he said. Pay off. Callan thought. Bit careless that. Someone's in a hurry. When the thin, sad geezer left, Callan followed him. Lonely was waiting for Davenport, and Callan was quite sure he wouldn't lose him.

The thin, sad one had a car: a bit of a relic but the engine was good. Callan had a hard time staying with him in the cab all the way out to the suburbs, but be made it all right, out to the semi-detached with the new paint glistening and the chrysanthemums just coming into bloom. There was a phone booth just opposite, and Callan used it. "Let me speak to Charlie, please," he said.

Hunter came on at once.

"I think we're on to something," Callan said.

The house next door was for sale, and that helped. Callan got his briefcase from the cab, then walked briskly down the path to the empty house, telling himself he was an estate agent. The front door lock hadn't been designed to cope with the kind of keys Callan carried. It yielded after the third kiss.

Callan went in, not hurrying, into the living-room, and opened the case. Typical estate agent's clobber: an A to Z, a thing like a stethoscope, and a loaded magnum .38 revolver with six spare rounds. He unfolded the thing like a stethoscope, fitted it to his ears, applied its end to the wall that separated the two houses, and found himself listening to a love-story.

The thin, sad man's name was Harry, and his wife was called Freda. They sounded neither witty nor attractive, but it didn't bother either of them: they adored each other.

At last she said: "I've got to go."

"Stay five minutes," he said.

"The kids get out sharp at four," she said, "and I've got the shopping."

"Take them with you. Buy them an ice-cream. My treat—here." Callan heard the clink of coins passed over.

"That's far too much," said Freda.

"Buy them something else then," Harry said. "It's time I gave them a treat."

"You sure you're all right?" she said. Her voice was a gentle mockery.

When she left Callan watched her from the window, and saw what he had expected to see: a woman approaching middle-age, who had learned to live with the problems of a mortgage, and growing kids, and never enough money; a woman who knew she was plain but it didn't matter; a man loved her.

He went back to listening, but the house next door was silent: Harry wasn't making any telephone calls. Callan waited for five minutes then left, walked up the path to Harry's door with the same brisk stride. A neat plaque on the door told him that Harry's surname was Miller. He pressed the bell, and a chime sounded. There was no answer. He pressed again — and again. No sound of approaching footsteps, no curtain twitching. This was bad.

Callan used his keys.

There was no one on the ground floor—just a note on the hall table, where she couldn't miss it. "To my darling wife." Callan raced upstairs. Not their bedroom: not the kids' room. The bathroom was the place. It had a sky light leading into the loft. You climbed up into the loft, screwed a pulley into a ceiling beam, ran a cord over the pulley, looped the cord round your neck and jumped down through the open skylight. Of course the force of it broke your neck, but at least you didn't choke to death. Callan looked at the grotesquely lolling head, hating the waste his trade created.

He went downstairs again, put on gloves, opened the note.

My Dearest Freda, when you read this for God's sake you and the kids stay downstairs and call the police'. Then a lot of stuff about how he loved her and how he'd once been in trouble, years before, and he'd been too ashamed to tell her. Only this man knew all about it, this man whose name he didn't know—and blackmailed him. Made him steal things from the Ministry *'because if I didn't he'd tell you—tell the kids. So I betrayed my country. I'd already betrayed you. At least I got some money for the things I've done—and it's yours, every penny. Forgive me Freda. One day you'll find a much better man than... Your loving, Harry.'*

Callan looked round for a briefcase, and there it was, worn and shabby, the property of H. Miller. Senior Draughtsman at the Ministry of Technology. He picked up the phone and dialled 9-9-9, asked for the police.

"Harry Miller," said Callan. "38, Acacia Drive."

"What about him?" the sergeant asked.

"He's dead," said Callan and hung up.

He left the door unlocked when he went back to the cab. He switched on the cab radio, called up Lonely.

"Where's our subject?" he asked.

"Still here, Mr Callan."

"I'm coming straight to you," Callan said.

But there was still one more call to make. Charlie had to be told.

"What do you make of it?" Hunter asked.

"He'd been up on a sex charge—a long time ago," said Callan. "Davenport was probably in court when it happened—and filed it away for future use."

"I think so too," said Hunter, "I'll have it checked. Where did Miller work at the Ministry of Technology?" Callan told him. "Exactly what our friend the cultural attaché was after. Better go and pick up whatever it was Miller gave him."

"I intend to," Callan said.

"There will probably be records of other unfortunates too," Hunter said. "Blackmailers are always greedy. Persuade him to give them to you then phone me again. I'll have him picked up."

"It'll be a pleasure," said Callan.

"Don't over-indulge yourself," Hunter said. "I want him alive."

Callan reached the West End at last, parked and walked to where Lonely sat in his cab.

"Still here, Mr Callan," said Lonely.

"Journey's End," said Callan.

"I don't get you," said Lonely.

"The job's over," said Callan. "So scarper. I'll pay you tomorrow."

"Won't I get to see what happens, Mr Callan?"

"You wouldn't like it," said Callan.

Lonely's voice rose to a squeak. "You mean there's going to be violence?"

"You can bet on it," said Callan.

File on a Chinese Hostess

"DO YOU like Chinese meals?" Hunter asked.

"Sometimes," said Callan.

"I'll buy you one," Hunter said.

Hello, Callan thought. Watch it. When he's generous he's deadly.

Nice meal though. Up West. The Middle Kingdom, it was called. None of your paper lanterns and Hong Kong plastic tablecloths. This one was all silken elegance and dim lighting and birds in cheongsams that walked you to your table and brought you hot scented towels and finger bowls.

Good-looking birds too. Slender and smiling, and walking with that trim elegance no Westerner can copy.

And the food was good too. Butterfly prawns and Peking duck and the kind of rice that crackled like a mini Guy Fawkes night. There was even a bottle of wine to wash it down. He *must* have plans for me, thought Callan.

Hunter finished his rice, handling his chopsticks with Chinese efficiency as Callan ploughed on with fork and spoon. A Chinese beauty brought more hot towels, poured the last of their wine, and left them.

"Like it?" Hunter said.

"Very much," said Callan.

"These young women—you find them attractive?"

So that's it, Callan thought.

"I'd need a psychiatrist if I didn't," said Callan.

"Perhaps you'd need one even more if you did," said Hunter.

"Which of them—turns you on—the most? Turns you on is the expression, isn't it?"

"Yes, sir," said Callan. "You've got it right." He looked round the room.

"The one in blue," he said. "Over in the far corner."

She was taller than the others and not quite so thin. The slit skirt showed long, impeccable legs and her black hair gleamed as if it were oiled. Nice eyes too, dark brown, not too slanted and with laughter in them. The mouth small and luscious. She would turn on a stone statue.

"Her name's Rose Li," said Hunter. "Twenty-three years old — so she says. Born in Hong Kong—so she says. No political affiliations—so she says."

36

"I gather the truth isn't among her attractions?" said Callan.

"She makes fifteen pounds a week and tips—and runs a flat in Knightsbridge and a very expensive sports car," said Hunter.

"Rich boy friend?" said Callan.

"Rich enough, Peter Arnold. Does the name mean anything to you?"

"No sir," said Callan.

Hunter sighed. "You must be without exception the most ill-informed member my section has ever employed," he said.

"I like to keep my mind clear for more important things—like staying alive," said Callan.

"Peter Arnold is a member of a textile family," said Hunter. "He is rich, single, and thirty-four years old. He is also Parliamentary Private Secretary to the Minister of State for Foreign Affairs." He waited. "Well, Callan?"

So he says it with chopsticks, Callan thought.

Aloud he said, "I suppose you're going to tell me Rose Li's an agent for Red China?"

"I am," said Hunter.

"But surely," Callan said. "Foreign Office security must be on to her? They can't be that stupid."

"They can," said Hunter. "But not this time. They've been on to her from the beginning. ... Three months ago. They called me up and asked me what to do."

"Left it a bit late, haven't you, sir?"

"No," said Hunter. "I don't think so. I advised them to do nothing—" he paused, enjoying Callan's amazement, "—except make sure that Rose Li got inaccurate information. They've had quite a jolly time apparently, feeding her a load of lies."

"Only now it's going to stop?"

"What makes you think so?"

"You've just bought me a Chinese dinner," Callan said. "But I'm the one who's going to pay for it."

"Perceptive as ever," Hunter said. "Her superiors feel rather annoyed with her—now that the information she passed on has been tested. They also think that she deliberately passed on lies."

"But how on earth could they?"

"I allowed them to think so. I also allowed them to think she's come over to us—gone double in fact. Our man in Hong Kong handled that. He did a quite excellent job."

He sipped his wine. "Her people will kill her, of course."

"And you want me to stop them?"

Hunter shrugged. "If it's possible. Don't take any chances on it. What I really want you to do is pick up her executioner. He'll be somebody quite good I imagine — they'll want her investigated first."

"And you want to interrogate the interrogator?"

"How well you put these things," said Hunter. "Oh, by the way— that's Arnold she's talking to now."

Callan looked across the room. Thin, clever-looking feller, and potty about her, he thought. Blimey, he must be.

"When's she due to die?" he asked.

"Probably tomorrow," Hunter said, "unless you can find time to save her."

Callan finished his wine and left, taking the route Rose Li must take to reach her home. If she used a cab or her car she'd be all right, but if it was a bus or Tube she'd have her problems.

It would be a piece of cake to lift her, take her somewhere quiet for a chat—then kill her. The flat was easy too—all mod cons—including a metal fire-escape straight to her back door. Callan looked at the lock on the entrance door. It was pathetic. He'd have to have the place watched—and by an expert. Whoever the Red Chinese sent would know his job. Time to call in Wun Big Smell.

"A Chinky?" said Lonely.

"That's right," said Callan.

"A Chinky bird?"

"Right again," said Callan.

Lonely hesitated. "All I got to do is watch, right?"

"That's all," said Callan. "When she shows up you light a fag. If there's another feller follows her—a Chinese feller—throw it away. And for Gawd's sake do it where I can see you."

"Where will you be, Mr Callan?"

"In her block of flats," said Callan. "Watching you. So do it right."

He got back to the restaurant in time to tail her home—her and Arnold. Very lovey - dovey, in Arnold's Bentley. Then upstairs into the flat, and the Bentley parked outside. And still there when his relief came, two hours later. How can anybody be that stupid, Callan thought?

But that wasn't his business. His business was to go home and sleep, wake and cook the biggest breakfast he could manage—there was no guarantee he'd eat again that day—then dress properly.

That meant a shoulder holster and a Magnum .38 with a silencer that he cleaned and checked for the thousandth time. Then in front of a mirror, and practise. Draw and aim, over and over, till arm and gun flowed into the smooth inevitability of death.

Or so you believed, thought Callan. But somewhere in the world there's another geezer who's even faster and trickier than you are. One of these days you're going to meet him—and maybe he's Chinese. Drop that idea. Get rid of it. Just draw and aim. And be sure you don't kill this one. He has to talk to Charlie.

His relief followed Rose Li to the restaurant, and Callan went in at noon. There was a bar there, and Callan looked at the five malts and nine blended whiskies behind it and ordered orange squash.

At 12.30 Arnold came in brisk and alert after his night of passion and began to read his newspaper. Fold it right and I could kill you with it Callan thought. And maybe somebody will.

Whoever's coming for her won't like you either, mister. Not when they know you passed on rubbish to her. And it won't be any good saying I didn't know. I'm sorry. Not when they start to hurt you.

Rose Li came up to Arnold and they talked softly together. Her voice was low-pitched, for a Chinese woman's, and with just a hint of sing-song. A bloody shame, thought Callan. All that beautiful femininity put at risk because Charlie wants to talk to a Chinaman. Ah well, lady. I'll save you if I can, but I'm not making any promises.

He left the bar when Meres came in. All day there'd be a succession of men and women from the Section in and around The Middle Kingdom, waiting, watching. But how the hell could you expect to spot one Chinese there? The place was stiff with them; diners, waiters, hostesses, cooks. He went to watch from a pub across the street. This was going to be a long and weary day.

She finished early that night — 11 o'clock, and Arnold wasn't with her. That was something Callan thought. Her flat wouldn't be the place for amateurs that night. He saw her into a taxi and watched a Section man follow her, then ran to where Danby sat on his bike, its engine roaring.

Danby was a mate of Lonely's, and he looked like a Martian in leather gear, but he knew how to drive that bike. They passed the taxi in nine seconds and reached Li's block of flats minutes ahead of her. Callan pushed a tenner into an unzipped pocket and Danby roared off.

That was the nice thing about Danby. He never asked questions, never said a bloody thing, come to that. Sometimes Callan wondered if he could talk at all, except to his motorbike.

He looked round the street in one comprehensive glance. Nothing doing so far. He walked up the stairs to the entrance and took out a key. Just as well no one was watching. This might take a little time, even though he'd made the key himself. It caught the ward of the lock, and slipped. Callan swore, and tried again. Slowly mate. There's no rush is there? People get killed when they rush. The key found the ward again, and held: the door opened.

Callan ran up three flights to the flight above her flat. Still nobody. Maybe he wasn't coming? Don't kid yourself, Callan, he's coming. And if it isn't tonight it'll be tomorrow. Sweet God let it be tonight— and get it over with.

He walked to the window and looked for Lonely. There were street lights and a moon just past the full and still it took him minutes to find him, even though he knew how the little man worked. When you're terrified, he thought, it helps if you're invisible as well....

Suddenly Lonely broke cover and lit a cigarette. I bet it's a dogend, Callan thought. He wouldn't waste a full one, not if he might have to throw it away. As he watched, her taxi drew up, and Meres parked further up the street. She paid off the cab and went into the flats and still Callan waited.

Lonely nursed the end of his cigarette and stepped back into a pool of shadow. *Funny business keeping stoppo for Chinkies. Not a bad looking bird though.*

A car drew up and a man got out. A Chinky, just like Mr Callan said. Lonely watched till he crossed the street and moved towards the block of flats, then stepped out of the shadow once more and flipped his cigarette end into the gutter.

Well, that was that. Another few bob earned—and a sight better than working. No sense in hanging about. Mr Callan didn't like you to hang about when the job was done, and besides, people sometimes got hurt when they met Mr Callan. Might as well go home. Down the street another car door slammed, and another Chinky walked over to the flats.

"Oh my Gawd," said Lonely.

Callan saw the little red arc of the cigarette stub, and moved down the stairs to a point just above Rose Li's door. The seconds went by, and he wiped his sweating hands. He mustn't fumble. This geezer will be good.

And he was. The Chinaman moved as softly as snow falls up to Rose Li's door. Didn't bother to knock, either. Just took out a key. Must have got it from her controller.

Equally silent. Callan's hand went to the Magnum's hard comfort.

The Chinaman opened the door, and Callan exploded into action. A straight lunge down the stairs, and his shoulder smashed into the man's back, knocking him down. The man whirled like a cat, his hand clawing for his shoulder, and looked into the blind, unblinking eye of the Magnum .38.

Rose Li came in from her bedroom. She wore black panties and a startled expression. Callan hardly saw her.

"Your gun," he said. "Take it out slowly." The Chinaman didn't move.

"I'll kill you," said Callan.

The Chinaman slowly took out his gun, and slid it towards him. As his left hand groped for it Callan said, "You'd better put some clothes on, love."

But she wasn't listening, which was absurd. Her mouth was opening in a way that meant she would scream. Callan flung himself backwards, and there was a whisper of sound above him: the Chinaman he had been covering suddenly had a knife sticking out of his left shoulder.

Callan rolled over and fired blind into the doorway. The Magnum popped and a second Chinaman fell on his knees by the door. He too wore a startled expression and had a second knife in his hand. It was he who had thrown the first knife. His target had been Callan.

Callan shut the door then looked at Rose Li. Her mouth was still open, but the scream wouldn't come.

"That buys me, love," he said. "Any time. Call or phone and I'll pay my debt."

"They'd come to—hurt me?" she said.

"To kill you," said Callan. "Now go and put some clothes on."

Rose Li looked down at herself and ran.

He looked down at the massacre. One wounded, and one—by the look of him—dying. Let's hope the right one was wounded. Time to call Charlie. He reached for the phone, and the doorbell rang. Meres's voice said. "It's Meres, Callan."

He opened up warily. It was Meres all right. With him was Arnold.

"I picked him up on his way to the door," said Meres. "We'd better come in. He's on to us."

Callan let them in. Meres looked around him with that regret he always showed when he'd missed a shooting.

Arnold's face showed nothing at all.

Callan said to Meres, "You'd better ring in."

Meres dialled the long, familiar number and said softly. "Let me speak to Charlie."

"You coped with them, I see," said Arnold.

"Just about," said Callan. "You know who they are?"

"Men sent to remonstrate with Rose for passing on false information, I expect."

"Men sent to kill Rose," Callan said.

Arnold shrugged. "No doubt she knew the risks she ran. I certainly did."

"You're saying you knew what she was up to?"

"All the time," said Arnold. "She was pretty obvious, you know. That's why I went to Hunter."

"I can't just take your word for it," said Callan.

"You can ask him. I'm surprised he didn't tell you already."

"Hunter's never blown a cover in his life," said Callan. "You had no business blowing yours."

"I'm hardly a professional at this game," said Arnold.

But you could be, you cold-blooded bastard, thought Callan. You even looked like a man in love.

"You were taking a hell of a risk," he said.

"It had certain—compensations," said Arnold.

There was a sound by the bedroom door. Rose Li stood there, dressed for the street, looking at Arnold.

Her eyes were still dark brown, and not too slanting, but they held no laughter.

File on a Willing Victim

"ANDREW HARDY," said Hunter. "Man of the Left."

Callan looked at the photograph. Wide-set eyes, sensitive mouth, one unruly lock of hair tumbling across his forehead.

Oh, blimey, thought Callan. Another intellectual.

"What's he done?" he said.

"Done? "Hunter considered. "He's written a lot of articles—and one book. He's the type who's always going to write another book—only the articles pay so much better he never has the time. Oh, and he does little bits on the telly as well. Witty pieces, you know the kind of thing."

"No," said Callan. "I don't. I only watch the cowboys. I mean, what's he done for you to give him to me, sir?"

"Ah," said Hunter. "I think we'll leave that one."

It's bad, thought Callan. It has to be. When Hunter won't even tell me.

"Someone's trying to kill him," Hunter said. "They've had two goes already. One with a car, the other — curiously enough—with a flower pot. Dropped from a great height, you know. Four storeys up, to be precise. It burst like a bomb."

"He can't be feeling too good," said Callan.

"He's feeling terrible," said Hunter. "After the flower pot he borrowed a house from a chum of his who's out of the country, and as far as I know he never leaves it. At least he had the sense not to send out a change of address."

"Do we know who's trying to kill him?"

"Indeed we do," said Hunter. "The H.V.A."

"East German Intelligence?"

"Exactly."

"East German Intelligence are trying to kill a man of the Left?"

"I agree it's odd," said Hunter. "But then so much of our business is extremely odd, wouldn't you say?"

"How Left is this Hardy?" Callan asked.

"He joined the party 15 years ago," Hunter said. "He didn't publicise the fact—but he joined."

"And now his comrades drop pots on him. What would you like me to do about it, sir?"

"I don't know," said Hunter, and Callan stared at him in amazement.

This was the first time he'd ever heard Hunter use those words.

"Go and have a talk to him, David. Tell him we can save his life—if he'll let us."

"If he'll let us?"

"I know, I know," said Hunter. "But I've talked to him already, you see. I told him we could save him—with absolutely no strings attached. He told me he wasn't interested, and I said in that case he would probably die."

"What did he say to that?" said Callan.

"I can remember his words perfectly," said Hunter. "He said. 'Of course I'll die. The H.V.A. are extremely good at their job.'"

"He's right, there," said Callan.

There was not much of a file on Hardy. Public School, Cambridge, degree in Economics; First in Part One, Second in Part Two. Good speaker in the Union, two good parts in Footlight productions, then London and journalism.

Write about anything this geezer. Economics was his special field, but he'd done the lot: space shots, cricket, opera — even rare china.

Lot of friends, but none really close. They included a lot of pinkos—you expected that—and a few real reds. No steady girl friend, but he wasn't queer. Travelled a lot: Romania, Poland, Czechoslovakia, East Germany.

Known girl friends in Czechoslovakia and East Germany.

Parents both dead; left him a bit of money. An officer and his lady. Callan wondered what they would have made of their son. At the bottom of the file Hunter had added a note in his own hand. "A brilliant sprinter, but totally unreliable over a distance."

Not the sort you'd need a gun for if you dropped in for a chat, but the H.V.A. were after him. Callan went to the armoury and drew a Magnum .38. If you had a Magnum and used it first the H.V.A. might just listen.

He went to the little house in Kensington that Hardy's chum had loaned him. It was painted white, but the paint needed cleaning. In the window boxes the flowers were half dead.

Callan knocked and rang, and no one answered, but he'd seen curtains twitch. He knocked and rang again and again. Over and over. Steady, persistent.

Hunter had said he wasn't a stayer, and Hunter was right. The door opened, and there he was: grey eyes, sensitive mouth, tumbling lock of hair—and drunk. Out on his feet at eleven-thirty in the morning.

"It's very boring when people refuse to go away," Hardy said.

"I find that myself sometimes," said Callan.

"I have no wish to buy encyclopedias, brushes, or subscriptions to magazines."

"And I have no wish to sell them," said Callan. "I'm from the H.V.A."

It was supposed to be shock treatment, and the shock part was perfect. Hardy just passed out then and there, and Callan had to move fast to catch him. Still, it got him inside the house. He put

Hardy on a sofa and went over the place. Nobody there except Hardy in the whole mess.

Hardy was doing the royal borough's image no good at all. The place was filthy: unmade bed with dirty sheets, the kitchen a circus for cockroaches; rotten food, empty bottles, stink and grease: even the study was neglected, the half-finished article on the typewriter abandoned in mid sentence.

He went back to the living-room. There was a case of whisky near the sofa: by the look of things Hardy had been taking his nourishment straight from the bottle.

It would take him hours to sleep this one off. Callan went back to the kitchen and the cockroaches, and brewed black coffee.

Hardy woke at three, the world was a hard place to come back to. His head hurt, his eyes watered, his mouth was dry.

But worse than the hangover was the fear that he remembered at once, and worse than the fear the anguish that even the whisky bottle could not drown.

Someone put a glass of fizzing liquid in his hand. He looked up, and the glass twitched, the liquid slopped on to his shirt.

"Get it down you," said Callan. "It's good for what ails you. Believe me, I know."

"You told me —" Hardy said.

"I told you lies," said Callan. "Get yourself in shape and I'll tell you the truth."

It wasn't easy, and it took a hell of a long time, but then patience was Callan's strength — the terrible, deadly patience that every hunting animal must have.

Hardy had nothing that could match that iron strength of will.

"I told another chap of yours," he said. "His name is Hunter—"

"Hunter's busy," said Callan. "I'm not. Why not tell me?"

"I don't want you and I don't need you," Hardy said. "Please go."

His hand reached for the whisky bottle, but Callan made him drink coffee: bitter, scalding, black.

"You may not want me," said Callan. "But by God you need me." No answer. "You told Hunter the H.V.A. were good at their job. Have you any idea how good?" Again no answer. Suddenly Callan's hand moved in one short, abrupt gesture, the Magnum flicked from under his coat, the barrel stared at a point between Hardy's eyes.

"I asked you a question," said Callan.

Hardy said unsteadily: "I understand that they are ruthless and deadly. So it seems are you."

"If you want to die I can't stop you," said Callan. "Nobody can. Even if you co-operate it'll be a slog to keep you alive."

"I want to die," said Hardy. "Can't you understand? I want to die. Please go."

"Tell me why first," Callan said.

"Because I deserve to," Hardy said. "I deserve to in a way that a Fascist like you could never understand."

Callan leaned forward, carefully removed Hardy's coffee cup from his hand, then hit him across the face, forward and back.

"I'm listening politely," he said. "Try talking the same way."

But even the blows it seemed were a punishment, and one that Hardy deserved. All he would do was mumble about betrayal of the proletariat, and a great light that failed.

"Come on," said Callan. "Words are your business. You can do better than that."

Hardy looked at him then: struggled for, grasped a certain dignity.

"People like me live idle, useless lives," he said. "We watch the death of a class-system that never benefited anybody but ourselves, and all we do is worry about our dividends—while all around us a new world is born, a better world for everybody. Even when we try to help that world, all we really do is hinder."

Oh mate, thought Callan. The number of times I've heard these words. Still you did say them as if you meant them. Aloud he said: "Try to stay sober, Mr Hardy. Don't make it easy for them."

"Drive a taxi?" said Lonely.

"That's right," said Callan.

"But I don't have a taxi, Mr Callan."

"I'll lend you one," Callan said. "Look son, don't get worried. It won't be anything undignified, like working. I promise you. You'll only have to take one fare."

"How long for?" Lonely asked.

"A day or two."

"How much. Mr Callan?"

"Fifty a day for as long as it lasts," said Callan. The little man hesitated. "Look son," said Callan. "Fifty a day tax free. Who else pays you that kind of money?"

"That's what worries me," said Lonely. "It's too much."

"What are you on about?" said Callan.

"It'll be dangerous, won't it?" said Lonely.

"I'll look after you. Don't I always?"

The smell came then and Callan pushed him away.

"Can't you buy yourself an aerosol or something?" he said.

"I don't think I want this job, Mr Callan," said Lonely.

"I'm going to pretend I didn't hear that," said Callan. "Now look at me when I'm talking to you."

Lonely stared up into Callan's eyes, then suddenly Callan's hands gripped his lapels, lifted him, feet dangling until their eyes were level.

"Now take your choice," said Callan. "Which do you want? A nice easy job or a belting from me?"

When Hardy left the house he was sober and quite sure he was going to his death. There was, he thought, no help for it.

The guilty must be punished and the innocent protected. So far he had failed miserably to protect the innocent. At least he had one chance to make amends before he died.

He walked down the street to an empty cab, gave the address and leaned back in the seat, wondering how death would come. But he couldn't compose his mind with thoughts of death.

His mind, he thought irritably, lacked seriousness even now. The damned cab smelt and he could think of nothing else.

Callan cruised along behind Lonely. Even terrified out of his mind the little man drove like a master: all his signals in good time, telling Callan exactly where they would go.

Nice part, too, out by the river, a big house with a formal garden. And barred windows and high, spiked walls. A nursing home would be the polite word for it, Callan thought, but the people in places like this were usually in for good.

Callan slowed, allowed Lonely's cab to draw ahead. Two men watching by the gate, two unobtrusive geezers idling the time away, having a chat, till they saw who was in the cab. Then suddenly they weren't idle any more.

Callan parked away from Lonely, then signalled the little man to scarper after Hardy paid his fare. The taxi took off like a Ferrari, and Callan joined a group of visiting relatives, following Hardy.

A nurse met Hardy, and they talked together as they walked down the corridor and reached a door.

Callan found a cleaners' cupboard and waited inside it till the nurse came from the room. He moved to the door and listened. Inside the room a television was going full blast, and above it was Hardy's voice, yelling in German.

Callan went inside.

Hardy was talking to a girl; perhaps the most beautiful Callan had ever seen. Blue eyes, golden hair, a perfect mouth: Hollywood's classic blonde.

No, not talking to her, yelling at her, striving desperately to reach that perfect beauty that would only stare at the antics of Hollywood gangsters on a 24-inch screen. He looked up and saw Callan.

"They've come for you," Callan said. "We have to get out of here."

"No," said Hardy. "I'm responsible for her. I won't leave her."

Callan shrugged, turned to the girl. "Do you want to get hurt?" he asked.

"She can't answer you," said Hardy. "She's — in shock. They don't think she'll talk again. Ever."

Callan took the girl by the hand, moved her away from the line of window and door. She went quite willingly — but her eyes never left the screen.

"Not here," said Hardy. "Even they wouldn't do it here."

"Why not?" said Callan. "It's the best chance they've got."

Hardy winced then, as if Callan had struck him again, then said unsteadily: "You'd better go. There's no reason why you should get hurt."

"Belt up," said Callan. "It's too late for me to like you."

He waited by the angle of the door, as gangsters yelled, motors roared, tommy guns chattered. Like living in a bloody nightmare, he thought, and looked at the girl, her eyes still on the telly as if it were her only reality....

The door opened briskly and two men in white coats came in, looking like doctors, except that each one carried a Makarov semi-automatic pistol.

One moved straight to Hardy, and Callan shot him dead, then dropped as the other fired on the turn.

A bullet slammed into the plaster above him, and Callan fired again, the impact of the bullet smashing the white-coated man down at the girl's feet.

A cop on the telly yelled: *"Come on out, Louis. You haven't got a chance."*

"In this game you make your own chances," said Callan.

He put away his gun, moved to the door, and looked back.

The girl's eyes had left the telly at last. She was in Hardy's arms, staring at the dead man at her feet. As Callan went down the corridor she started screaming.

"A bit messy," said Hunter. "It is in every paper in the country."

"I'm not," said Callan.

"Of course you're not. Hardy didn't even know who you were. And anyway—he's grateful to you. He'll keep his mouth shut."

"So that's something else we owe him," said Callan.

"I don't think I understand you, David," said Hunter.

"I think you understand me very well—sir," said Callan. "Hardy did a job for you in Dresden, didn't he?"

"What makes you think that?"

"I heard him talking to the girl in German. He did a job and the girl helped him. Only Hardy got away and she didn't. They interrogated her—and when they'd finished they'd damaged her mind so she couldn't even speak.

"But even then they had a use for her. Hardy loved her, so they sent her here, used her as bait. They knew Hardy would go to see her—and when he did they'd kill him."

"Hardy set up Gelber for us," said Hunter. "The best spy-catcher in East Germany. When I had him killed he was hours away from two of our agents. A cautious man Gelber. But naturally he trusted Hardy—a party member. One of their own."

"What did you use on him? "Callan asked.

"After Czechoslovakia, Hardy had a crisis of conscience," said Hunter. "It wasn't too difficult to persuade him that if the Czechs were right the East Germans were wrong."

He paused "Hardy really is grateful to you, you know. That German girlfriend of his has got her voice back. In time she may get her mind back too."

"We owe them that much," said Callan.

"Dear me," said Hunter. "That sounds like conscience. Don't you start having a crisis of conscience."

"How can I?" said Callan. "I work for you."

File on a Kindly Colonel

COLONEL Obra was 34. That was young for a colonel, even in the army of an emergent West African nation, but Colonel Obra was good at his job, and popular with the people and the Government.

If he stayed that way he would be Prime Minister by the time he was 40, and knew it.

If his popularity slipped he would be dead. Colonel Obra knew that too.

He didn't like London. It was cold, it knew nothing about his people and their struggles, and it was much too far away from his country, where moods and Governments changed so fast.

But it was necessary to be here, to bargain and make deals: for money, machinery, armaments: the things his people needed. What his people needed was always paramount for the colonel.

He got up from his chair and walked across his office. In the anteroom a man was waiting: the man the British insisted he had to have. A bodyguard—and a good one, they said. His name was Callan. His own personal white gunman. Not bad going for a one-time corporal of police.

"I have a luncheon appointment," Colonel Obra said.

"Yes, sir," said Callan. "At the Three Lilies."

"You have a table too?"

"Next to yours," said Callan.

Obra smiled.

"Your work and mine both have their compensations," he said.

Callan thought: I wonder who wants to kill you? You're big and charming, you're a treat to work for and the best hope your country's got. But somebody wants you dead or Hunter wouldn't have put me here. Let's hope I can stop them—whoever it is. For both our sakes.

Obra walked out and Callan followed behind, a little to Obra's right. They walked down the stairs of the pretty Belgravia house.

Below, Obra's wife was waiting, and Keino, his A.D.C. Mrs Obra was brown and beautiful: a new bride. She and Obra had married only six weeks ago.

A hell of a way to spend a honeymoon, thought Callan. But she seemed able to cope with it. She was as bright as she was beautiful, and took diplomats, bankers, industrialists, in her stride.

Obra adored her for it. Nobody adored Keino. He was black, American-educated, and consumed with hatred for anybody white, but he was a hell of a hard worker. He had to be, with Obra driving him.

Keino went to the door as Obra appeared—opened it and signalled. The Mercedes 600's doors opened, the chauffeur stood ready. Callan went to the door, and Keino didn't move: he never did.

Callan had to push him aside.

"Let me see the street," Callan said.

"Yassuh, boss, anything you say boss. I hear you boss," said Keino.

"Belt up," said Callan.

Behind them, Obra chuckled. This was a daily ritual, and he never failed to enjoy it.

They went down the stairs and into the car, Mrs Obra beside the chauffeur. Obra sandwiched between Keino and Callan.

"The Three Lilies," said Obra.

"Very good, sir," the chauffeur said.

Funny what a good chauffeur Lonely could make when he had to, Callan thought. He even got the voice right....

Hunter detested visiting Whitehall. The men he had to see there despised him and his trade, and made little effort to conceal the fact. But that didn't stop them yelling for him, whenever they needed help, and forgetting about him completely as soon as the need was over.

Sir Robert Dundee was the worst of the lot: looking at him as if he were a road sweeper with something very nasty indeed in his shovel.

"You've got a man on Obra?" Sir Robert asked.

"Yes," said Hunter.

"A good man?"

This was insolence, but Hunter let it pass. There were things he needed: things that only Sir Robert could give him. He would wait till he got them.

"Good enough," he said.

"Let us hope so. It could be very awkward indeed if Obra were to die."

"The possibility still exists then?"

Sir Robert flushed a savage, unpleasing pink. Too much port, thought Hunter, and not nearly enough exercise.

"Of course it exists," Sir Robert said. "I told you—"

"On the telephone, ten days ago. I put a man on Obra immediately. The best man I've got. But you haven't told me what you know."

"Obra's prime minister has cancer. He may die at any time," Sir Robert said. "He's kept it quiet so far—but he had to have a specialist to see him. I sent him one—faked up an excuse about organising a new hospital.

"The prime minister talked his head off to him—the only one he has talked to. If the P.M. dies, Obra takes over—provided his talks with us are a success. And provided the Left don't get him first. If they do, the Chinese walk straight in."

"You have a file on all this?"

"It's extremely confidential," Sir Robert said.

"Aren't we all?" said Hunter.

*   *   *

Callan looked up from his *sole dieppoise*. At the next table the colonel and his wife made polite conversation with a banker and an industrialist, and Keino sulked because they were white. Situation normal.

"This came for you, sir," the waiter said.

Callan looked at it. Foolscap-size envelope. OHMS. Stuffed full by the look of it, and with it a second, smaller OHMS envelope. The big one was marked "Colonel Obra." The smaller one "For the attention of David Callan. Esquire Most Urgent." Callan opened it

And read from Commonwealth Office headed writing paper.

Dear Mr Callan, Please convey the enclosed to Colonel Obra the moment he is alone. It is for his eyes only. (Signed) *Robert Dundee.*

Sir Robert. The twit who had got Hunter into this thing.

"Who brought these?" Callan asked. "Is he here?"

"No, sir. The gentleman just said it was for the man at the table next to Colonel Obra and left."

"Gentleman? A Negro gentleman?"

"No. sir," the waiter said. "Just a gentleman. He wore an Old Etonian tie. Funny that. He didn't look like an Old Etonian."

"We don't always you know," said Callan.

The waiter left.

Callan picked up the larger envelope. Inside there were papers all right, but inside them was something else, something hard and unyielding.

Callan started to sweat. Easy now, don't panic yet. This thing'll be fixed to go off when you tear the flap and not before.

He signalled to his waiter again.

"My bill, please," he said.

"You haven't finished your lunch, sir," the waiter said.

"I seem to have lost my appetite," said Callan.

Walking out of the restaurant was the hardest thing he had ever done. The envelope seemed to weigh about a ton, and it seemed to be ticking. But that was ridiculous. Whatever it was had to be plastic, and plastic doesn't tick.

He could see the surprise in Obra's eyes, the hate in Keino's as he passed them, but the best chance he had for them was to keep walking.

He reached the street looked down the line of parked, cars. Meres was there on standby. Callan walked up to him.

"Go and take over," he said.

"Suppose he asks what happened to you?" asked Meres.

"Tell him I feel sick," said Callan, and looked at the envelope. "It's the truth."

"Well, well, well," said Hunter. They stood behind the blast wall and

50

waited while the explosives expert, with infinite care, fixed a fuse to the envelope and ran it slowly back to them.

The envelope rested on a table between two dummy figures and one of them, Callan thought, looked far too like himself. The explosives expert reached them and set down the fuse.

"A bit crude, sir," he said, "but I gather you're in a hurry."

"I am," said Hunter.

The explosives expert lit the fuse and a dot of fire ran along it, up the table leg on to the table.

"I should put your heads down now, gentlemen," the explosives expert said.

The sound when it came was a single hard crack: it was the light that hurt, so white and searing that even behind the blast wall Callan thought he had gone blind. The expert looked up.

"Nasty," he said, "very nasty."

Callan stared at where the bomb had been. The table was reduced to a heap of lumber, burning fitfully. The two dummies were shapeless plastic blobs. He turned away, retching.

"I told Meres I felt sick," said Callan. "I wasn't kidding."

"He's with Obra?" Hunter asked. Callan nodded. "He'd better stay there for the moment. I want this thing stopped, Callan. I want you to stop it."

"I'll be glad to," said Callan. "Any leads?"

"Dundee has a doctor contact with Obra's P.M." said Hunter. "There was a pretty strong left-wing opposition till Obra got rid of its leaders. The new ones all went underground."

"Names?"

"He doesn't have any. I'm not surprised. Obra's a very ruthless chap."

You should know, thought Callan.

Aloud he said: "The Commonwealth Office envelopes and paper. No fingerprints. I suppose?"

"Only yours," said Hunter.

"Who could have got hold of them? They looked genuine enough."

"They were. But half Obra's staff have been in and out of the Commonwealth Office. There was a press conference there last week, remember?"

I remember, thought Callan. They were all over the place—and who would bother watching a man with Mrs Obra to look at?

"Find him, David," Hunter said. "Find him and put him away. But do it quietly. No fuss. I don't want a diplomatic incident any more than Obra does."

* * *

"Plastic?" said Lonely. "I've always been a jelly man myself when I had to be. Crude stuff it is, noisy."

"Never mind gelignite," said Callan. "I said plastic. Think."

Lonely sucked at his tea and looked round the kitchen. Nice place. Nice job, come to that, driving a big Merc. Cushy. He didn't want to think of plastic. Dangerous stuff. You could get hurt.

"You don't need to do a job, Mr Callan," he said. "You got one. This body-guarding lark."

"Somebody tried to do a job on me," said Callan. "If it had worked you could have eaten me with chips."

The smell came.

"Gawd," Callan said. "Don't you ever run out of fragrance?"

No. That wasn't the way. The little man was petrified with terror. He tried again, more gently.

"Look, mate," he said. "It's over. All I want is the geezer who did it. Now are you going to help me or not?"

"I better make some phone calls," said Lonely.

It took five, and at the end of them Callan had an address.

"Ta," he said. "Now there's just one more thing I want you to do."

"I don't want to get mixed up in this," said Lonely.

"Not even for money? Fifty quid for one simple job."

"I might get hurt," said Lonely.

"Turn me down and you can bet on it," Callan said. Slowly, patiently he told Lonely what he must do.

But first he had to call on the man who could get you plastic. It wasn't a pleasant interview, and Callan hadn't expected it to be. In the end Callan had to choke him with his Old Etonian tie.

After that the man who could get you plastic was only too willing to talk, once he'd got his voice back.

Callan waited till he'd been given the name he wanted then knocked him unconscious, remembering only just in time to hold back on the blow. This geezer handed out packets of plastic like Christmas cards— and he didn't give a damn who got hurt, provided he got paid.

Callan willed himself back to calmness and dialled the long familiar number.

"Let me speak to Charlie, please," he said. Hunter came on at once.

"Charlie here."

Callan gave him the address. "You better send some coppers," he said. "And tell them to mind how they go. There's enough stuff here to blow up Birmingham."

"Have you got a name to work on?"

Callan told him.

"Good God," said Hunter. "Just how do you propose to handle that?"

"I don't," said Callan. "I'm going to give it to Obra. It's his problem."

He went back to the house in Belgravia. The time had come to finish it. Whatever came out of it would be nasty, but it would be up to Obra how he handled it. There wouldn't be any diplomatic incidents, not if Lonely got it right.

He found Meres in the ante-room, looking bored. From behind the doors of Obra's study came the murmur of voices.

"Feeling better, old chap?" said Meres.

"I'll live," said Callan. He looked at the door and his hand flicked up, inside his jacket, to the hard comfort of the Smith and Wesson's butt.

"Good Lord," said Meres. "We are touchy today."

"Who's in there?" Callan said.

"The colonel and his lovely bride. And that bird Keino. He's not lovely at all. Do you know—I don't think he likes even me?"

"You'd hardly think that was possible," said Callan. "Listen—I've got a job for you."

Meres listened at once. Work was a serious business: the only real passion he knew.

Callan knocked at the door and went in. The strain of Obra's work was beginning to tell. Or maybe he'd caught a smell of how close he was to death.

Whatever the reason, the lines on his face looked deeper than Callan remembered—but he smiled as Callan entered.

"Ah David," he said. "I hope you're feeling better."

"I'm fine now, thanks," said Callan.

He looked at Mrs Obra, impassive behind her beauty, then at Keino, furious that a white man should interrupt when black men settled their destinies. Callan kept his hands in full view of all three of them.

Come on, Lonely, he thought. Come on.

But the little man was bang on cue. He tapped at the door, and walked up to Callan. He even managed his posh voice.

"Excuse me, sir," he said. "You left this downstairs when you came in."

He handed Callan a foolscap envelope marked OHMS.

"It's for you, sir," Callan said, and moved to Obra.

Mrs Obra rose and picked up her handbag.

"I think I'll arrange some tea," she said.

Callan blocked her off as Obra took the envelope.

"I think it's for you too," said Callan.

She moved forward again.

"Let me pass please," she said, and her hand went into her bag.

"Callan — what the hell—" Obra began, then stopped.

His wife's hand came out of her bag. In it was an automatic.

"It's a pity," she said. "A bomb would have been better." Her eyes moved to her husband. "But you'll feel it, Obra. You won't die easy."

From the door there came the soft plop of a silenced gun, and the automatic was jerked from her hand across the room. She screamed with the pain of it.

"I'm most awfully sorry," said Meres. "One was brought up never to shoot at ladies."

Callan talked and Obra listened, then went to question his wife. He moved like an old man, but his face was still determined. When he came back his face showed nothing at all.

"She's been a Red ever since college," he said. "Her instructions were to make my talks fail—if necessary by killing me. Tomorrow my talks will succeed."

"She's alone in this?" said Callan.

"Here—quite alone. She gave me other names back home."

"You're sure?"

53

Obra looked at him.

"She didn't lie to me," he said. "Not this time." He picked up the automatic. "I think you and Mr Meres had better take a little drive in my Mercedes with my chauffeur. I have a domestic matter to arrange."

In the car Meres said, "What do you think? A shooting accident?"

"It could be," said Callan. "That's the trouble with guns. When people start fooling about with them—they go off."

File on a Chelsea Swinger

"LIKE HER?" Hunter said.

Callan looked again at the photograph. A neatly rounded figure, elegant legs, a pretty, cheeky face under a smooth and shining cap of yellow gold hair.

"I'd be queer if I didn't," he said.

But the eyes bothered him. They were beautiful eyes, but they'd seen too much for a bird as young as this—and it showed.

"Her name's Sarah Vane," said Hunter. "At least she says it is. She lives in Chelsea. One of those blocks of flats named after impossible plants—Fuchsia Lodge. Sounds pretty ghastly. As a matter of fact you'll be living there yourself. She's twenty-three. Married and separated. Lives well—nobody quite knows on what."

"What's she done?" Callan asked.

"*Done?*" Hunter sounded surprised. "Nothing."

Callan forced himself to speak patiently. "What file's she in then? Yellow?"

"Sort of a natural shade," said Hunter. "She's clean as far as we know."

Callan struggled even harder to maintain his calm.

"Then may I ask, with respect, *sir,* why you're showing her to me?"

Hunter laughed, an indulgence he allowed himself perhaps three times a year.

"My dear boy, didn't I tell you? Someone's going to kill her."

"Anybody we know?"

"The KGB," said Hunter, and Callan's calm became at once a part of himself. Never get angry when the KGB was involved: that was a certain way to die.

Hunter said: "The French had a defector last week. Called himself a trade counsellor at the Russian Embassy in Paris. In fact, he was a cipher clerk for the KGB. He didn't have access to much, but he photographed what flies he could and ran.

"One of them had the Vane woman's name on it. When they debriefed him they asked him why she was there. He said she was marked for death—so they asked him why.

"He said he didn't know—why, or how. He had no idea. All he knew was that it would happen two days from now."

They're always so bloody certain, Callan thought, even the defectors.

If the KGB say you'll die—then you'll die. Unless Hunter puts Callan in the way and his luck holds. When it runs out – maybe you'll both die....

"I take it the Russians don't know about the photocopies?" Callan said.

"The French rather think not. It was quite neatly done. Any ideas?"

"Paris," said Callan. "It's funny this should turn up in Paris. ... You're sure that's all the French could tell you?"

"It's all they would tell me," said Hunter. "There are times when I detest the French." He sounded like Henry V before Agincourt.

"It could be a contract," Callan said. "It's not all that hard to hire a gun in Paris these days and some of them are good."

"But why on earth should they? Their own killers are superb."

"Suppose he bungled it—whoever it is. Suppose we found out who it was—and were able to prove it? It would be a bit embarrassing for the French, wouldn't it? Just when we're trying to be nice to each other. And if he did a good job, they've still got their kill—they might even shop him to us after it's over. Either way they win. They like that."

Hunter nodded, as if impressed, but Callan knew he'd been on to it all the time.

"Splendid, David," he said. "Now go and stop it happening."

Callan took the information on Sarah Vane and read it with great care, talked to the men who had dug it out for Hunter, and sent them to dig even deeper.

Sarah Vane had been born in Stoke-on-Trent, twenty-three years ago, but then she'd been called Annie Woods, She'd come up to London when she was seventeen, worked in a bank and loathed it, dropped out and reappeared as Candy Kissen, a Soho stripper in a club called Nudissima.

Eighteen months of that and she'd married Alasdair Trenton Vane, sixth in line to a barony, daddy a merchant banker. Then they'd split up, and she lived happily ever after—till the KGB got around to killing her.

Soho and Chelsea, Callan thought. Chelsea was where the leopard would hunt, but Soho was for rats, and for rats you needed a terrier. An ageing terrier maybe, and more than a little smelly—but the best nose in the business. He went to call on Lonely. It was time the little man had a treat.

For Lonely a treat meant fish and chips and beer, and after that a cowboy picture. When Callan suggested the strip-club, he shied like a curate.

"I don't know, Mr Callan," he said. "I mean it's nice of you to offer—"

"You don't like them?"

"I didn't say that now, did I?"

Callan looked up at him. Lonely was blushing. It would have been so easy to take the mickey—and so stupid. He needed the little man.

"Better if you don't like it," Callan said. "I want you to keep your eyes open. This is work, old son."

"Work?" said Lonely. "Watching strippers?"

"You'll earn it," said Callan.

So Lonely stayed where he was, and Callan went south to the King's Road, and Fuchsia Lodge, which wasn't nearly so bad as Hunter had threatened—if you liked Italian furniture.

Callan was the ultimate square and, even in his best Italian suit, he looked like Mr Cube's last stand.

He picked her up outside the flats, tailed her to an Indian restaurant, then on to a discotheque where they had a bar with a mirror that made life easy. All he had to do was look in the mirror and keep track of the men who came up to her table.

Callan went to the phone. It was time Lonely had left Nudissima and gone home. The little man said: "I had a bit of luck, Mr Callan. The barker's an old mate of mine. Name of Bolger. We done bird together."

"He was there when that Candy Kissen was an artiste. He showed me some pictures. You should see them, Mr Callan."

Apparently Lonely didn't embarrass by telephone.

"I can imagine," said Callan.

"Only she looked—nice," said Lonely. "Not like the others—scrubbers they was. Still are, come to that."

"You find out why she left?"

"That Vane geezer you mentioned—he'd been chatting her up for weeks. She upped and married him. Bolger wasn't half surprised."

"Why?" said Callan.

"He'd never got around to talking marriage before."

Callan sold softly: "Before what, you stupid burke?"

"Sorry Mr Callan. I wasn't concentrating."

"Then start concentrating," Callan said, "before I get mad." For one wild moment Callan thought the smell was coming through the phone.

"Yes, Mr Callan. Before this night – April it was, a Thursday. She did her last show, went off, and came back on Friday to collect her duds—what there was of them. She got married by special licence the next week."

"That's better," said Callan. "You're doing all right."

"Thanks, Mr Callan."

"Twenty quids' worth," said Callan. "You can make it fifty if you want to."

"Course I—"

"Find out what else happened near the club that night."

"Like what, Mr Callan?"

"How the hell do I know? Anything unusual."

"Like violence, you mean?"

"Could be," Callan said.

"I don't like violence, Mr Callan."

"You'd better remember that," Callan said.

* * *

When he got back to the bar, Vane was with her. A man a little hesitant in his movements, but sleek with the polish that only money brings.

Getting to her was largely a matter of timing, but then so was killing a hired gun from the KGB. Callan waited till Vane stood up and turned to speak to a friend at the next table. He had his glass in his hand.

Slowly Callan threaded his way between the tables. As Vane began to turn back to his own table, Callan moved and Vane, so it seemed, collided into him and poured a great deal of gin and tonic over his Italian suit.

"My dear chap," said Vane. "I'm most awfully sorry."

"That's all right," said Callan.

"Oh but it isn't," said Vane, and began to mop at Callan's coat with a napkin. From close up he seemed, Callan thought, to be much more drunk than hesitant.

"I must buy you a drink," said Vane. "A very large drink."

He signalled for a waiter, and Callan found he had a Scotch he could have launched a tanker with. Vane had a bottle of gin, two-thirds empty. The girl had abandoned gin for cola.

"My name is Alasdair," Vane said. "Alasdair Vane. This is Sarah. She's more or less my wife."

"David Callan," Callan said.

"We haven't seen you here before, have we?"

"No," said Callan. "I've been away." He sipped his Scotch.

"Why don't you dance with Sarah?" Vane asked. "I'm a bit beyond in. I'm afraid."

"I don't dance," said Callan. "I just like to watch."

"Really?" said Vane. "That's very interesting Sarah and you have an awful lot in common."

He began to laugh them a loud and uninhibited laughter, and maybe that was what finished him. When the laughter died he said: "If nobody minds I'll pass out," and did so.

Callan watched the girl. No disgust, no outrage, just a tender regard for Vane and embarrassment for himself.

"I'll help you get him home," said Callan.

Home was in the next block to theirs, and when they had laid Vane on his bed Callan walked back with her to Fuchsia Lodge. She turned at the door and held out her hand.

"Thank you so much," she said, in her best debutante voice.

"I'm coming in too," said Callan, and saw at once the shrewd, survivor's look in her eyes.

"I live here," he said.

She laughed then, and it was all easy, now that he was a neighbour. They could have coffee together, and they could talk, and Alasdair wouldn't mind because he'd been damned decent. She talked for half the night, about Stoke-on-Trent, and the hardships of living in London — but not about strip clubs — and about how absolutely super Alasdair was.

"What does he do?" asked Callan.

"Alasdair? Nothing. He's just—rich. It's lovely."

"Did you say you were married?"

"We are," she said. "You mean we don't live together. He won't—just now. It's his drink problem you see—when he's beaten it—."

She smiled then. The promise in her smile was infinite.

It's a tough world for Cinderallas. Callan thought. Even when Prince Charming does come along he turns out to be an alcoholic—and she draws me for Dandini. He left her at last; shy and polite and gentlemanly—and she almost kissed him. Later he was glad that she didn't.

Next morning he called Lonely again, and he was big with news. The night Candy Kissen had left the strip-club to become Sarah Vane there'd been a murder in the court behind the club.

"Anybody done for it?" Callan asked.

"No," said Lonely. "It was a real professional job—I wouldn't want to be mixed up in it. Mr Callan."

"You won't be," Callan said. "As of now you're unemployed. Pay day Friday—see you then. And thanks old son."

"You're very—welcome, Mr Callan."

Then he called Records at headquarters, hung up, dialled the long, unlisted number and asked to speak to Charlie. Hunter listened, questioned, and at last agreed. Time to get up then, eat breakfast, read a while till Records called back, then lie down and relax. Sleep if you can. Don't think about food—or drink. Not till the job's over. Just relax.

At six he got up, bathed, shaved, and dressed: old suit, old shirt, and an old and totally reliable Smith and Wesson .38 Magnum: the only friend he could trust. Before he left, he phoned Charlie once more.

"You knew all the time what she saw, didn't you?" he asked.

"I suspected—no more," Hunter said.

"Try suspecting there'll be some survivors tonight," said Callan.

Hunter sighed: "Very well. Bring them in and I'll talk to them."

* * *

She opened the door and was pleased to see him till he pushed past her, locked the door and searched her flat, then told her what was going to happen.

"Kill me?" she said. "You're crazy."

"Not yet," said Callan.

"But why on earth should anyone—."

"Because you saw a man commit murder—and you can recognise his face."

The words hit her like blows and she was a long time recovering.

"You a copper?" she asked at last, and the debby accent was dead.

"Sort of," said Callan.

"Then why don't you take me to somewhere safe?"

"There's nowhere safe till I kill him," said Callan.

She looked at his eyes then, with a hard courage he admired.

"Then you better do it," she said at last.

"We may as well talk while we're waiting," he said, and the questions began, the ones he had been trained to ask, and slowly, reluctantly, the answers came at last. She fought hard for Vane, but he was too strong for her. Records had given him all he needed.

"His family had cut him off. He didn't have a penny till you told him what you'd seen," Callan said. "He got it then from the K.G.B.—for keeping you quiet. They didn't mind paying—two more murders were a bit strong—even for them."

"Then why kill me now?"

"The murderer's name was Orlov. He's left the K.G.B. now—being groomed for the big time—the Politburo. You might see his picture in the papers."

"Alasdair didn't tell me that," she said. "He told me it was some Soho gang. That they would hurt me."

"The dead man was a Czech," said Callan. "He had information for us—stuff that might have helped a lot of Czechs to get out—if Orlov hadn't got him first."

"But how would Alasdair know all this?"

"We think he'd been used before," said Callan.

At two in the morning the doorbell rang and Callan hid behind the door. It was Alasdair, and when she let him in he was cold sober, but carrying a bottle.

"Darling," he said, "I hope you don't mind but I've asked a friend of mine to join us. As a matter of fact I gave him my spare key."

Behind him Callan said, "Your friend's a murderer, Vane. What does that make you?"

Vane spun round, swinging the bottle, and Callan hit him once, slow and easy, and caught him as he fell.

"Violence is vulgar," Callan said. "And anyway you drink too much."

He put him on the sofa, out of the line of the door, and she went to him. Callan turned off the lights and waited with the iron patience that was his greatest strength, the Magnum with the silencer in his hand as the time crawled, and at last the door opened, and a small, neat man eased into the room, as silent as still water.

"*Bonsoir, Monsieur*," said Callan, and the small, neat man whirled: the silenced gun plopped with a noise like a champagne cork. The small, neat man fell like a stone, a Colt target pistol still in his hand.

A butterfly gun—unless you're accurate. Callan thought. He must have been good. He turned to the girl.

"You believe me now?" he said, and she nodded. Her eyes had lost their shrewdness now.

"Alasdair," she whispered.

"You want him?" She nodded once more. "You can have him for me, love."

"What—will happen to us?"

"You'll have to speak to Charlie, then we'll see," said Callan. He bent by the dead Frenchman, took the target pistol out of his hand.

"*Adieu, monsieur*," said Callan.

File on a Missing Poet

"A POET?" said Callan.

"They do exist," said Hunter. "This one's name is Digby—R. E. Digby. Ever heard of him?"

"No," said Callan.

"He's rather a good poet," Hunter said. "He even makes money at it. Here's his picture."

Callan looked at it. Strong face — about thirty-five by the look of him. Clear eyes and a no-nonsense jaw. Neat suit. No beard or beads either. Not on this geezer.

"He looks like a tough bank clerk," said Callan.

"And acts like one—most of the time," said Hunter.

'But he is also—so I'm told—a genius. Are you sure you never heard of him?"

"Positive," said Callan. "What's he done? Written an ode to Lenin?"

"He's another of those awkward ones," Hunter said. "He hasn't done anything—except go on a visit to Moscow. His books sell very well in the East—in fact he's almost a rouble millionaire."

"Well good for him," said Callan.

"Of course he can't get his money out—so he goes over there and spends it. Vodka, women, and caviar, I gather."

"Lucky old R. E. Digby," Callan said.

"He went over to Moscow three weeks ago," Hunter said.

"Usual pattern: parties with students, a few drunken evenings with Soviet poets—and a rather pompous weekend at a dacha owned by some critic or other. Our Number Two in Moscow was there too. He had a list of names—rather an important one. The names of the people in the Politburo who are in favour of an H-bomb attack on China—should the need arise. We'd rather like to know who they are."

"I rather thought we would," said Callan.

"Our Number Two had the list in microdot," Hunter said. "He was well aware that the K.G.B. were getting close to him—and he had the room next to Digby's. Poor chap—the K.G.B. picked him up the day after Digby left."

"Alive?" said Callan.

"Unfortunately yes," Hunter said.

Callan blacked out his mind to what had been done in Moscow to a man whose name he didn't even know.

"How long would he stay quiet?"

"Our psychological people give him three days. Frankly, I think that's rather generous."

"So do I," said Callan. "Nobody could take three days of that."

"As it happened, one would be enough if our guess is right and he planted the microdot on Digby. The poet took the next Aeroflot flight to Paris."

"You want me to pick him up there?" Callan asked.

"That would be absolutely splendid," said Hunter.

"Unfortunately, we don't know where he is. All we know for certain is that he arrived in Paris a week ago—and he hasn't been home since. He could be anywhere. I want you to find him, Callan — and get hold of that microdot before the K.G.B. do."

Find a poet. Sounded like one of those damn fool organisations you see in the yellow pages. Rent-a-scribe. Where the hell did you start? Read the collected works? He bought them and got a receipt for them. Accounts tended to be fussy about literature.

"They have a special quality," the salesgirl said. "A sort of dark power."

Callan looked at the poet's photograph on the back. *You mean R. E. Digby has love,* thought Callan.

He tried Archives. They had nothing, but they put people on to it. The wheels turned. In clubs and pubs, editors, critics, publishers, were bought unexpectedly large drinks by chaps they hadn't seen for ages, and Callan learned that what he had feared was true: R. E. Digby had a host of girlfriends, and knew half the B.B.C. and the whole of Fleet Street, but he had no special friends apparently.

The break came from the watch Callan had asked for on Digby's house: a neat little semi in the suburbs with a lawn as well-barbered as those of his civil servant neighbours.

A young woman let herself in with a key and tidied up, and one of the watchers tailed her home. Callan thought he might as well take a look at the house too—and then at the woman. It was time Lonely did a bit of professional work: it would never do to let his fingers get stiff....

"A poet?" said Lonely.

"A poet," Callan said.

"Blimey," said Lonely. "There was a young feller from Wapping."

"Belt up," said Callan. "This is literature."

"You mean there's money in it?"

"There is for you if you do it right."

"I've always been a good steady worker, you know that, Mr Callan. It's just...I never heard of a bent poet before. What's his game?"

"It's better if you don't know, old son. You'd only worry."

"Mr Callan—there won't be any violence, will there?"

"Put it this way," Callan said. "You won't see any."

Lonely shuddered, but his work that night was as good as ever. They went in as if they'd had invitations. The house itself was as tidy as the garden, but the furniture had nothing to do with suburbia: a five-seater settee in soft leather, a canopied bed, a huge circular bath.

"He looks like a geezer who enjoys hisself," said Lonely. "When's he got the time to do all that reading?"

He looked round him. The house was stacked with books. In the study, the bedroom, even the bathroom.

"Let's go and ask somebody," said Callan.

"Who, Mr Callan?"

"A bird," said Callan.

"What bird?"

"Miss Angela Cosgrove," said Callan. "Lecturer in Comparative Literature at the University of Surrey."

"A lady teacher?" said Lonely. "I never got on with my teachers—always clouting me they were. Anyway, what would she want to talk to us for?"

"Because we'll persuade her," said Callan.

At once there came the smell.

"You said no violence," Lonely said.

"I said you wouldn't see any," Callan said. "I meant it. Come on."

She had a flat in Leatherhead, but she wasn't in it. Once again Lonely broke in, sweet as a nut, no mess, no complications, and they looked around. A nice flat, good pictures, easy furniture, a display table with a collection of snuff-boxes.

Callan left Lonely to keep watch by the window, and want over the rest of it. Books, more books, a pile of manuscript poems; original R. E. Digby. And very nice too, if he meant all he said about Miss Angela Cosgrove, M.A.

Callan went back to the living-room and looked at the snuff-boxes. Lonely had never been able to resist a snuff-box in his life. The things had a fascination for him, like aniseed to a dog.

"Put it back," said Callan.

"Put what back, Mr Callan?"

"The box you nicked."

Lonely sighed the sigh of a man ill-used. "I thought this was a job," he said. "Some job when you can't even nick a—."

"Belt up and put it back."

Reluctantly the little man did so, then his eyes wandered to a photograph.

"That can't be her," he said.

"It is," said Callan.

"Stone me," Lonely said. "Schoolteachers has changed since my day."

And, indeed, Miss Cosgrove was, by any standards, pretty. She had character too, by the look of her. A stand-no-nonsense quality that reminded Callan of Digby.

The trouble was, Callan thought, there'd be a good deal of nonsense before he found out if she had anything worth telling. He sat down and waited for Miss Cosgrove.

Waiting was what he was good at. He had to be. In his game the one who could wait the longest usually won.

"She's coming," Lonely said. Callan looked at the little man. His eyes were pleading.

"O.K.," said Callan. "You can scarper."

So when she came in, brisk, assured, there was only Callan there to greet her. Lonely was already half way down a drainpipe.

She took it well. The fear was there, but she controlled it.

"If you've come to steal," she said, "you should have found out about university salaries."

"I don't know whether I have or not," said Callan.

"Who are you?"

"A poetry lover."

She looked bewildered, wary and prettier than ever.

"R. E. Digby's poetry," said Callan.

"You don't look mad—or drunk," she said. "I'll make a bargain with you. If you leave now — I'll promise not to tell the police."

As she spoke she backed off to the door. Callan waited till she had almost reached it, then moved in a sudden eruption of speed.

His arms reached out to her—and she found she couldn't move. No man had held her with such a lack of feeling for as long as she could remember.

"Listen, Miss Cosgrove," said Callan. "Just listen, I'm going to tell you a bit about myself then you're going to say that's ridiculous, and we can start from there."

He told her enough about who he was and what he did.

"That's preposterous," she said.

"Preposterous is even better," he said. "But I think you believe me."

She twisted in his arms and looked at him. "Yes," she said, "I do." He let her go then. "But why come to me?" she asked.

"Because you know Digby."

"Are you telling me that Ronnie's a spy?"

"No," said Callan. "He's a poet. We all know that. But he's also a messenger – and he doesn't even know that himself."

"You mean you used him?"

Callan nodded. "Because he was handy."

"But why him? You could have got him into terrible trouble."

Callan said: "He is in terrible trouble. But it could get worse if we don't find him. Do you know where he is?"

"No," she said, "I don't. And if I did I wouldn't tell you. You have absolutely no right."

"The man who gave your boyfriend his trouble is in Lubyanka," said Callan. "If he isn't dead. I hope he is dead, Miss Cosgrove, because Lubyanka is run by specialists and what they specialise in is pain."

He told her some of the things he knew would have been done to Hunter's Number Two in Moscow. When he had finished: "My God," she said, "I believe you, I really do. It's ghastly, and Ronnie..."

"Tell me about him," said Callan.

"What can I tell?" she said. "I've known him six weeks." *Fast working Digby.* "I'm going to marry him. He doesn't know it yet – but I am."

And she means it, thought Callan. *That's why she hates me.*

"Who are his friends abroad?" he asked.

"How can I possibly know? He hasn't written to me since he left Moscow. We've only met five times. There's been no chance to find out about each other."

He nearly missed it.

"You mean he wrote to you in Moscow?"

She nodded. "He sent me a letter – a friend of his in our embassy brought it."

"Let's see it."

"No," she said, "I won't. It's private."

"Nothing's private in this game, darling," said Callan.

"I don't care," she said. "I won't."

Just as well Lonely left the room, thought Callan. If he was here I'd have to ask him to close his eyes. Seeing a woman hit upsets him ... and all for a ruddy microdot.

Then he remembered the poems Digby had sent her. She had a mole on her left hip.

Digby seemed to see a deep spiritual significance in it—and a hell of a lot of satisfaction. A small mole. Not much bigger than a microdot.

He found what he was looking for on the third one. The dot over the "i" in the word "hip." Hunter's Number Two in Moscow had a sense of the fitness of things—while he lasted. She swore and tried to scratch when he took the letter, and Callan again exerted that impersonal strength.

As he held her, the doorbell rang.

Callan said softly: "Expecting anybody?"

She shook her head, and the doorbell rang again. Callan let her go, and she moved at once to the door. Deftly he tripped her into a chair.

"Wait," he whispered.

There was silence more ominous than any sound, then a key grated in the lock.

Callan's hand made a smooth, inevitable movement and the silenced Magnum appeared.

"No," Miss Cosgrove said. But the word was a whisper, her eyes stared in terror at the magnum's barrel.

From outside the door a man's voice said, "Angela, are you there?" And that it seemed was all it took. She bounced to her feet.

"Ronnie," she said. "Oh, Ronnie!"

The door burst open then, and Callan flung himself prone as an eminent poet with a surprised look on his face was hurled into the room.

Behind him were the two men who'd done the hurling: business-suited geezers with bowler hats, one of whom was carrying a Makarov semi - automatic pistol instead of an umbrella.

The magnum popped, and the bloke with the Makarov fell.

Callan moved his gun a fraction to cover the other geezer and he froze, his hand inside his coat.

"Come on in," said Callan. "Make yourself at home."

65

The geezer came in, and Callan rose, clouted him with the gun-barrel, and took away his pistol.

"What the hell is all this?" said R. E. Digby.

Callan looked at the man he had shot. He was dead all right — there hadn't been time to worry about winging him—and he still wore his bowler hat.

In life he had been dangerous, even deadly: death had turned him into a clown.

"I think I'll let Charlie tell you that," said Callan. Still holding the Magnum, he picked up the phone.

*

"It seems Digby had gone to Provence," said Hunter. "He'd told some people in Moscow he might, so the K.G.B. had no trouble in picking him up there. The two chaps you... er... dealt with, told him they were book dealers. Said they wanted to buy the original manuscripts of his latest poems. Offered him quite a lot of money. That's why he took them straight to Miss Cosgrove's flat. He was quite annoyed when he found that it wasn't true."

"Why didn't he ring her first?" said Callan.

"They persuaded Digby it would be amusing to surprise her," Hunter said.

"She was surprised all right," said Callan. "But I don't think she found it amusing."

*

So there it was: a nice, tidy operation, except that something was missing, Callan brooded alone in his flat and sipped his whisky, and suddenly remembered. He reached for the phone.

"Listen," said Callan. "That limerick."

"That what, Mr Callan?"

Callan willed himself to patience. *There was a young fellow from Wapping,*" he said. "How does it go on?"

Lonely told him.

"You naughty little rascal," said Callan.

File on a Friendly Lady

"LIKE her?" Hunter asked.

Callan looked at the photograph of the blonde, and knew at once that it didn't do her justice. This was a blonde who could debauch a bishop.

"You could say that," he said.

"Or there's this one," said Hunter. "She's quite attractive."

Another picture, another bird. A brunette this time. A lot more aloof than the blonde, but just as easy to look at.

"You could say that too," said Callan.

"I want you to look after them," said Hunter.

"I want me to look after them," Callan said. "What have they done?"

"Nothing that we know of," Hunter said. "The fair one's name is Mrs Harper—at the moment."

"At the moment?"

"So far she's been married three times," Hunter said. "I gather she's considering it again. The other lady is married to Mrs Harper's brother. Her name's Mrs John Francis."

"And they want me to look after them?"

"No," said Hunter. "I want you to do that. They will probably resent it—especially the fair one. I understand she's rather wild."

"That's fine with me," said Callan.

"They are Americans," said Hunter. "They will be staying at the Savoy. So will you."

"You expect to rough it in this job," said Callan.

"Mrs Francis's husband is a United States senator," Hunter said. "John Francis. One day he may well be President."

"Is he here, too?"

"Not yet," Hunter said. "He may join them later."

"Two gorgeous birds over here on their own and me at the Savoy looking after them? Where's the catch, Hunter?"

"So far as I know there isn't one."

"You're joking," said Callan.

"We both know that's impossible," said Hunter. "I merely suggested to Senator Francis that we keep a friendly eye on his wife and sister. He was delighted that anyone should volunteer to keep an eye on his sister. There is one other small thing."

I knew there would be, Callan thought.

"Mrs Harper's current boy-friend. His name is Grant. He's English but he spends a lot of time in the States. He's an amateur photographer," said Hunter. "Photographers always intrigue me."

"Of course they do," said Callan. "They take pictures."

"Keep them out of trouble—and keep out of it yourself," said Hunter. He passed Callan a yellow file—surveillance only.

"And carry a gun," said Hunter.

"On a surveillance job?"

"The senator asked that you should—he's very fond of his wife and sister."

"Blimey, he must be," said Callan.

Mary Lou Harper, the file said. Born 27 years ago in Atlanta, Georgia. She and her brother between them owned about a tenth of the State. Married first to a ski instructor, then to an oilman, then to a TV actor. Divorced each time. Reason for divorce: incompatibility—each time.

Current boy-friend: Peter Grant. The file had nine pages on him, but what it boiled down to was that he took photographs at a loss and women at a profit.

The file didn't say much about Susan Francis, which meant that there wasn't much to say. She was 25 years old and had been married to Senator Francis for a year. She was rich and intelligent, and never in trouble. Mary Lou was never out of it, except when Susan was around. Mary Lou, it seemed, would do a lot for her sister-in-law.

*

They met over tea. Lapsang Suchong, thin china, *petits fours*. The gun under his coat had never felt more ridiculous. Nor had he.

"Well, ah do declare," said Mary Lou. "Ah've finally got me a bodyguard."

"Isn't he cute?" said Susan.

"Ah feel safe all over," Mary Lou said.

More than I do, Callan thought, and tried not to look at her long, sleek legs. The two women went on with their innocent fun.

"Susan, honey," Mary Lou said, "do you realise—if we didn't have Mr Callan here to take care of us we might have to cross the street on our own?"

"Is he good at crossing streets?" Susan asked.

Callan stirred his tea and tried not to sweat.

The trouble was that the pair of them were so damn good at it: building up a picture of a fumble-footed halfwit who thought he'd had a good day if he crossed a room and didn't knock anything over.

They kept it up through tea, a walk along the Embankment, dinner in a restaurant and a night-cap in their suite. I don't blame them Callan thought. They're big girls now and they don't need a nursemaid. But why not take it out on Hunter—or Senator Francis? Why pick on me? When he got up to leave he felt about 15 years old and covered in warts.

68

"Goodnight, Mr Callan," Susan said. "You've been a good sport. Thank you."

"I've been a good loser," Callan said. "With you two it's just as well. Goodnight."

He walked to the door and Mary Lou crossed over to open it.

"Goodnight honey," she said, and grinned at him. "You know—Ah don't see why you should lose all the time."

She kissed him on the mouth then, her body firm in his arms, and turned to Susan.

"He's a good winner too," she said.

Callan enjoyed the kiss but was under no illusions why he got it. Now she knew he was carrying a gun.

Next day was a nightmare of shopping. Both women appeared to be inexhaustible, and as playful as ever. When Callan escorted them across Bond Street, Susan said triumphantly: "I knew I was right. He can cross a street." When Mary Lou bought a bra she said to him. "You see—honey—we're different from you—and when you're all grown up and everything, you'll want to find out where. And honey—Ah know you won't believe this now—but it'll be fun."

Then there were the jewellers, the antique shops, the furriers. Dazedly Callan remembered asking Hunter what the catch was. He knew now.

At a cocktail party at the American Embassy, Mary Lou told a polite, bewildered African that Callan could balance a biscuit on his nose, then Susan begged the African earnestly not to let Callan do it; he always got crumbs on the carpet.

They kept it up at Belinda's the supper-club discotheque where Mary Lou wanted to eat supper and Susan didn't — but agreed to go anyway. Callan thought it was the noisiest place he could remember outside a foundry, but at least it was the place where Susan stopped making fun of him.

She stopped when a man came over to join them; a man called Peter Grant. Callan listened to Mary Lou's squeal of delight that he'd left Palm Springs, and Grant's talk of amazing coincidences, and knew that Grant lied. He'd followed her to protect his investment, and who could blame him? *A good body and a handsome face doesn't last for ever, so he fusses over her and is jealous of me.* It was obvious that Susan hated him for the fuss he made of Mary Lou and her teasing stopped. Callan found to his astonishment that he missed it.

"How marvellous to run into you here," Grant said and signalled a waiter to bring another chair.

Callan waited till he sat on it, then said: "Won't you join us?"

Mary Lou laughed. The two men were so aware of her, and of each other. *She likes that*, thought Callan, *but at least she's not telling Grant what I am.* Grant took her off to dance and Callan caught the scowl on Susan's face.

"You don't like Mr Grant?" he asked. She gave no answer.

"Mary Lou does," said Callan.

"You're wrong," she said. Callan noted the tension in her voice.

"I heard she was going to marry him," said Callan.

"You heard wrong."

When the time came for Grant to ask Susan to dance she got up at once. Callan thought civilised behaviour could sometimes be too much of a strain. He thought it again when Grant arranged to join them for lunch the next day.

Grant bothered him. It was not the cool arrogance of the stud, or the gracious way in which he allowed Callan to pay the bill. The man was too sure of himself.

He and Mary Lou weren't even engaged yet and Callan had learned already that the last thing you did with Mary Lou was take her for granted. Yet the man acted as if he controlled the whole scene.

Callan left them to make a phone call and when Grant tore himself away at last, he had company. Not company that he would want or even tolerate if he knew of its existence. But that was the point. When Lonely tailed you, you didn't know.

Callan was taken to choose more bras and didn't see Lonely again till six. It had taken all his powers of persuasion to see him at all. The little man was terrified of the Savoy even when he'd put his best suit on. It aggravated his problem considerably. Callan sniffed as he let him into his room.

"Have trouble did you?"

"No Mr Callan, nothing like that," said Lonely.

"Why are you so niffy then?"

"It's this place," said Lonely. "I don't know how to go on here."

Callan thought of Mary Lou.

"I know what you mean, mate," he said. "Tell me about Grant."

"He's got a service flat in Bayswater. Nothing flash," Lonely said. "Bit of a dump really. Nothing like this place."

"You're getting to be a connoisseur," said Callan. "Here's what I want you to do."

He talked and the little man listened carefully.

"But I don't even know what pictures to look for," he said at lat.

"Neither do I," said Callan.

"Suppose there aren't any pictures?"

Callan remembered Hunter's voice: *Photographers always intrigue me...*

"There'll be pictures," said Callan.

"It would be a help if you was coming with me," Lonely said.

"But, mate, I can't," said Callan. "I'm lumbered with a couple of birds."

"Wish I could get lumbered like that," said Lonely.

As he left, Mary Lou's door opened, and she appeared. That night's cocktail party was at the French Ambassador's and she was dressed accordingly.

"Why David, honey, you've got a friend," she said, and smiled at Lonely.

"Gawd blind O'Reilly," Lonely said, and fled.

From the party they went to another discotheque, where Peter Grant joined them. Callan waited for a couple of hours, then got up to go.

"Why, honey," Mary Lou said, "you aren't leaving us all unprotected?"

"Don't worry," Callan said, and smiled at Grant. "I'll be back in time to pay the bill." Then he threaded his way through the dancers and was gone. From the next table Meres gave no sign that he had seen him go.

Lonely was waiting in a car parked near the hotel. Being a car that Lonely had borrowed, it smelled but not too badly. The job must have gone well.

"No trouble?" said Callan.

"No." The little man was contemptuous, almost indignant. "The locks in them places is a disgrace. Might as well leave the door open."

"What d'you get?"

Lonely handed it over, a heavy steel cash box already opened and inside it two thousand dollars in tens and a roll of prints, pictures of Susan at a party. She looked doped and beautiful. She also looked naked.

"All right, isn't she?" said Lonely.

"She's going to be," said Callan, and put the prints back in the box. "Where's the negative?"

"There wasn't one," said Lonely. "Honest."

"Don't use words you don't understand," Callan said. He gave the box to Lonely.

"Put it back," Callan said.

"Put it back? But I've only just nicked it," said Lonely.

"Put it back," said Callan. "*Now.*"

It was time to call Hunter.

After that he went back to the discotheque, and paid the bill. Getting rid of Grant wasn't easy, but Callan enjoyed it. Back in their suite Callan said to Susan. "I didn't know you were a nudist."

Mary Lou was on to him at once. "Are you crazy?" she said.

"Not me," said Callan. "I think she was." He moved to Susan.

"I saw the picture Grant took of you in your birthday suit," he said. "How much does he want for it?"

Breaking people can take months or minutes. It depends what you hit them with—but when they do break. It's always terrible to watch. Susan crumbled at once. She'd been to a pot-smoking party just once in her life, the pot had worked only too well, and Grant had been there with his all-too-candid camera.

"How much?" Callan asked.

"Five hundred dollars a month," said Susan. "But—"

She hesitated, and Mary Lou said: "Go on, honey. You can trust Callan."

"I daren't," Susan said.

"Honey, you must."

"He says he doesn't want money any more. He wants—information. Things my husband knows."

"Have you done that?"

"Not yet," said Susan. "He's sending another man to see me—tomorrow."

71

"You took stuff—from your husband?" She nodded. "Without telling him?" She nodded again.

"I had to," she said. "Politics is Jack's whole life. If that picture came out he'd have been ruined. He'd hate me."

"Have you got the information with you?" Callan asked.

Again she nodded. "I won't tell you what it is," she said.

You don't have to, Callan thought. Hunter had a searcher on his way here the moment I rang in tonight.

He turned to Mary Lou. "You were on to Grant?"

"Ah had my suspicions," she said. "That's why Ah let him get so friendly." She turned to Susan. "Why didn't you tell me?"

"I love Jack," Susan said. "I don't want to lose him."

"Maybe you won't," said Callan. "What else did Grant tell you?"

"He said the other man he's sending would give me the negative if I gave him the information," Susan said. "Do you think he's lying?"

"No," said Callan. "They usually do that."

"Usually?"

"For God's sake," Callan said. "Do you suppose you're the first one? Grant's joined the big boys now."

"How big?" Mary Lou asked.

"The KGB, by the look of it. This is routine stuff for them. They'll send a heavy to you tomorrow, and he'll give you the negative—if you give him the stuff he wants. But Grant will hang on to the prints for the next time—unless I take them from him."

"Ah see now why you carry a gun," said Mary Lou.

"Yeah," said Callan. "You've got to be careful when you cross a street."

Next morning Susan sat alone in the drawing-room of their suite, till the door opened and a waiter came in, pushing a trolley-load of breakfast. He was deft and competent, but his jacket didn't quite fit, in an hotel where everybody's jacket fitted perfectly.

The waiter's eyes flicked round the room and saw everything, including the fact that Mary Lou's door wasn't quite shut. He bent forward, too quickly, to lift a cover from a dish, and Callan kicked the door wide and fired once, then again, the silencer making a noise like champagne corks popping in an hotel where it's never too early for champagne.

The waiter died with a gun in his hand. Warily Callan stooped and searched him. In his pocket was the negative: no prints.

He called Hunter then, and told him to send the cleaners, then went to Grant's flat. Grant was big, and he'd learned a few tricks from somewhere, but he wasn't Section trained. It didn't take long. When he'd finished. Callan was sure he'd got all the prints, and Grant wasn't nearly so handsome as he had been. Even Meres, when he came to take Grant to Hunter, was impressed.

Callan went back to the Savoy for the last time. Susan was asleep. Mary Lou had given her a sleeping pill, and now gave Callan champagne.

"You're so damn good at it," she said.

"I have to be," said Callan.

"We owe you a lot," said Mary Lou.

"Susan owes you something too," said Callan. "You covered for her pretty well."

"I love her," Mary Lou said. "So does Jack. And anyway — nobody cares what I do."

"You're wrong there," said Callan.

Mary Lou said again. "We owe you a lot."

Not so much as you think, thought Callan. Meres photographed one of those prints for Hunter, and he'll use it—if he has to. But he didn't say it aloud. The lady was busy—and it wouldn't have been polite to interrupt.

File on a Jolly Miller

"INTERESTING face, isn't it?" said Hunter.

Callan looked at the picture again. Interesting wasn't the word he'd have chosen himself. It was the kind of face you'd expect to see on a chubby parson who's just been passed the port. Friendly, cheerful, full of good will. Maybe that's what made him interesting.

"His name's Miller," Hunter said, "or Muller when he's in Germany, or Millet when he's in France."

"Travels a lot, does he?" said Callan.

"On occasions. He's a freelance."

"He looks pleased with himself," Callan said.

"He has reason to be. In the last seven years he's made over £300,000. Quite soon he hopes to make even more."

"Lucky feller," said Callan.

"That's rather up to you," said Hunter. "I want you to make sure that his hopes are unfulfilled."

"What's he up to them?"

"He's about to steal a tank," Hunter said.

"A bit dodgy—sneaking it out of the works under his coat?"

Hunter sighed. Callan was an excellent agent, but life would be much more tolerable if only he would stop making jokes.

"He is employed as a draughtsman," Hunter said. "Over the past six months we believe he has successfully photographed the drawings of our latest tank—the Hero. Soon he will sell the photographs—."

"And live happy ever after?"

"As I say—that's rather up to you."

"Who's buying?"

"East Germany," said Hunter. "They set up the whole operation. It's taken rather more than two years."

"The Israelis pulled the same gag with the Mirage fighter," said Callan. "It worked."

"It's your business to see that it doesn't happen this time."

"Yeah. You keep telling me," said Callan. "How did you get on to him?"

Hunter said bitterly, "You may well ask. He radioed Dresden three days ago to tell them he was ready to do business—and one of our monitoring operators recorded the message by mistake. He actually came in to me to apologise."

He scowled as Callan began to smile.

"It took us 36 hours to break the code, and the best part of a day to

74

get a line on him. If it hadn't been for a sheer accident he'd have been and gone and we wouldn't have known a damn thing. What the devil are you laughing at?"

"Damned if I know," said Callan. "If it hadn't been for a sheer accident. I wouldn't have to pick him up." He paused, then said. "Why me, Hunter?"

"Because," Hunter said, "he's a very difficult man to arrest."

Callan looked again at the jolly, well-fed face. "Slippery, is he?"

"Dangerous," said Hunter.

"Him?" said Callan.

"Him. With a pistol he is both fast and accurate."

"As good as me?"

"It's difficult to assess that kind of information, but for what it's worth I should think he's at least as good as you—probably better."

Blimey, thought Callan. And I was laughing.

Hunter gathered up the photograph, put it in its file, and gave the file to Callan. It had a red cover.

"I see," said Callan.

"I think you do," said Hunter. "The man's a menace. Get rid of him. But first I want those photographs back—and his East German contact whoever that is."

"You don't want much," said Callan.

"Don't be absurd. I want everything. I always do," said Hunter. "And when I don't get it, I'm extremely displeased."

Getting the photographs meant breaking and entering, and for that it was necessary to take the advice of a professional man. The professional man he needed was eating fish and chips, standing up at the counter of a fish bar. Callan came up soft-footed behind him, put on his coppers voice. "I want you," he said, and Lonely seemed to shoot up in his raincoat like toothpaste in a tube. He spun round to face Callan, spraying chips.

"Mr Callan, that's not nice," he said.

Callan sniffed, and moved back.

"You're telling me," he said.

"You're only got yourself to blame," said Lonely.

"You're so right," said Callan. He thought of Hunter, and then of Miller.

"My sense of humour will be the death at me," he said. "Fancy a job?"

"In my state? You may have had your laugh, but I'm a nervous wreck, Mr Callan."

It took three pints of bitter to calm him down, and after that they drove out to the suburbs where Miller lived, just five minutes by bus from the design office which produced the plans for the Hero tank.

Callan parked the car and disguised himself as Mr Tucker of the Civil Service. To do this he put on a raincoat and carried a briefcase, and with them the kind of form-filling, penny-pinching manner that belongs only to official snoopers.

He walked briskly up the garden path to the little semi-detached house and rang the bell. As he waited, he looked at the lock on the door. A Manton, triple-action by the look of it. There were no better locks in the world. Burglar alarm leads too, and steel mesh in the ground floor windows. Mr Miller knew his stuff.

The door opened on a chain, and callan could just see Miller's face and shoulders. Something about the set of the shoulders told Callan he had a gun in his hand, but the face was beaming like a bishop announcing a Christmas treat.

"Mr Miller?" said Callan.

"Yes?"

"My name is Tucker—Ministry of Housing. There are one or two questions I must ask you."

Callan opened the briefcase and pulled out a form.

"It's in connection with your PY83."

"I don't think I've had it," Miller said.

"Good heavens," said Callan. "It should have been completed by now. Perhaps if I were to come in and help you with it —"

Miller hesitated, then somewhere at the back of the house a dog barked.

"I'm sorry," said Miller, still beaming. "It isn't convenient at the moment. Come back some other time."

The door started to close. Callan thrust the form into his hand.

"Very well," he said. "I shall call tomorrow for the completed form."

He walked up the street and distributed a few more PY 83's to indignant house-holders. He sympathized with their indignation, but Miller might be watching, and from what Hunter had told him people who took chances with Miller didn't live very long.

When he got back to the car Lonely was already waiting. Callan looked at his face. It didn't even need that long, sad shake of the head to tell him they were on a loser.

"It's a tough one, Mr Callan," said Lonely. "The back of his place is like a ruddy fortress. Even a tank couldn't get in there."

You're wrong there mate, though Callan. There's a tank in there right this minute. Our problem's to get it out.

"Two triple action Mantons," said Lonely. "And there's a dog in there, too."

"I know," said Callan. "I heard it."

"Yeah and I seen it," said Lonely. "And I don't want no part of it Mr Callan, thank you very much."

"Big, is it?" Callan asked.

"Like a bleeding rhinoceros," Lonely said, then proceeded to harangue Callan on the churlishness of people who distrusted their fellows so much they went in for Manton locks and dogs with teeth like bandsaws. "I don't know what the world's coming to, Mr Callan," Lonely said. "I don't really."

Then suddenly he twisted round and looked behind him.

"That geezer set the coppers on to follow us," he said.

"Don't talk wet," said Callan.

"Well somebody's following us," Lonely said.

Somebody was. A neat, professional shadowing job, never coming up close enough for Callan to find out who it was.

Callan dropped Lonely off and went on to a pub for one slow, cautious whisky, making it last, till a girl came in to buy cigarettes, swirled round in a movement as arrogant as it was pleasing, and spilled what was left of it all over him.

She apologized prettily enough and bought him another, and took a campari for herself. Nice blonde hair that owed nothing to a bottle. Innocent blue eyes. And you can do a beautiful tailing job in a car darling, Callan thought. It's a treat to have you following me.

He told her his name was Tucker and that he was a civil servant, and the girl somehow, contrived to convey that all her life she had wanted to meet a civil servant called Tucker.

"My name's Lund," she said. "Christina Lund. I'm from Berlin." The part with the wall around it, thought Callan.

They talked a little longer. Then they both discovered they were hungry, and thought they might as well have a bite together since they had become such good friends so quickly. Over the meal she did a good job of pumping information from him too—about his job, and his friends, and the work he did. It was as well, thought Callan, that he'd been Mr Tucker for years.

She was as thorough as she was subtle. She even got it out of him that Mr Tucker and his colleague Mr Renfrew had been out distributing PY 83's that very evening. Lonely in the Civil Service was a thought to conjure with, but Callan ignored it and told her instead about forms and schedules and in-trays and out-trays till the poor girl clenched her jaws to stop herself from yawning.

Tucker must be the most boring man in the world, thought Callan, and went on talking to the end. After the meal he offered her a lift, but her own car was quite near, and Callan walked to it with her, and told her about inter-office memos. The girl got into the car as if it were a lifeboat.

"You think she believes you're Tucker?" Hunter asked.

"I was beginning to believe it myself," said Callan.

"We put a tail on her last night as soon as you rang in," Hunter said. "She went straight back to Miller's place. Since neither of them have run away, we can assume you were convincing. I'm having the house watched, of course."

"She's there to collect the film?" Callan asked.

Hunter nodded.

"Then why doesn't she just take it and go?"

"She'd like to, I'm quite sure," Hunter said. "But she can't. Not till the money's been paid to a bank in Geneva, according to Miller's radio signal. He'll wait for a telegram. When it arrives she'll get the film."

"And we move in," said Callan.

"Precisely," said Hunter. "How many men will you need?"

"Just Meres," said Callan.

"How do you propose to get inside?" said Hunter.

Callan said: "That's rather up to Mr Tucker."

He looked at Miller's file again. The dog was allowed out for exercise three or four times a day—but it never left the garden. Callan wondered how good Meres was with an air-rifle. Immobilising the dog was their only chance of getting in quietly.

He found Meres in the duty-room, as polished and elegant as ever. "I've got a job for you. Toby," Callan said. "I want you to tranquillise a dog."

"Oh God," said Meres.

Getting Lonely to agree to go back wasn't easy.

"All you've got to do is open the back door and let a mate of mine in," said Callan. "I'll keep him busy while you're working."

"I'm not saying. I couldn't do it. Mr Callan, Lonely said, "but you never seen that dog."

"We'll fix the dog. I keep telling you," said Callan.

"You couldn't fix that dog with a sledgehammer," said Lonely.

"I could fix you with a sledgehammer," Callan said. "Now belt up and get your keys."

The little man sighed and pulled up a floorboard in his room. Beneath it was his collection of keys and picklocks.

"You sure you'll fix the dog, Mr Callan?" he said.

Meres waited in the back of a van parked near Miller's house. It was hot and uncomfortable, and no van which contained Lonely could ever be called fragrant; but he waited in silence, and his concentration never wavered. At last the door was opened by a pretty, blonde girl, and the dog came out into the garden.

"Let's hope she doesn't rush to tell Miller what she's done," thought Meres, then slowly, carefully, rested the air rifle on the van's half-open window, and waited again till the dog lay on the grass. Slowly, carefully still, he aimed and fired. The dog yelped and brushed with his paw at one shoulder where the tiny dart had hit him.

"You got him," said Lonely. "What happens now?"

"That's rather up to Callan—and you," said Meres.

"You only want me to open the drum, right?" said Lonely. "You don't want me to hang about."

"I never want you to hang about," said Meres.

Suddenly the dog stopped scratching and slumped down yawning, making no move when the boy came with the telegram, yawning again as Mr Tucker, brisk and efficient as ever, arrived soon after. Meres hoped to God that Miller couldn't see the dog from the house.

Callan walked up the path and rang the bell, and once more confronted Mr Miller, looking even jollier than before.

"I've called about that form I left," said Callan.

"Of course," said Miller. "I have it here." He handed it to Callan, and began to close the door.

"If I might just check it through," Callan said.

"Of course," said Miller.

"Could I come inside?" said Callan.

Miller smiled more broadly than ever. "No," he said.

Callan took his time reading the form, and hoped to God Lonely was working fast on the back door.

At last he said: "That seems satisfactory," put the form in his briefcase and turned to go.

From inside the house Christina Lund's voice called: "Miller—look out."

Miller started to slam the door shut, but Callan stuck his brief-case in the gap as it closed. Again the girl's voice yelled, and Miller moved back, calling to the dog, then ran back into the house. Callan pushed the door open, drew his Magnum, then went in a flying dive, through the hallway to the kitchen where Christina Lund stood over the body of Meres. Miller, smiling once more, aimed a gun at Callan, and Callan knew that his luck had run out at last.

It was the dog that saved him. It shambled into the room behind Callan, its drugged mind still responding to Miller's call, and leaped at the intruder as it had been trained to do, knocking Callan flat as Miller fired, taking the bullet in its own brain as Callan fired back and Miller fell. Christina Lund looked into the magnum's unwinking eye and was still.

"I was wrong about you," she said.

"A lot of people are," said Callan.

He flicked a glance at Meres. "You killed him?"

She shook her head. "I just knocked him unconscious, that's all," she said.

I wish I could have seen that, thought Callan, then looked from the dead dog to its dead master.

"You were lucky," the girl said.

"That's right," said Callan. "If our chemist had got the doses right, the dog would be unconscious and I'd be dead—and you'd be on your way back to East Germany."

Meres groaned and stirred. In his hand was a roll of film. The girl looked at it as if it were the most important thing in the world, and for her it probably was.

"You could still be lucky," the girl said.

"Could I?"

"Very lucky—if we do a deal."

Callan shook his head.

"My Government was going to pay Miller a quarter of a million for that film. It could be yours, Mr Tucker."

"I'm sorry," said Callan, "Deals aren't my department."

File on a Deadly Doctor

"AMERICANS are incredible," said Hunter. "Quite incredible."

Callan made no answer. Hunter could bitch about Americans by the hour, and all it meant was that somehow or other he was in debt to the C.I.A. for something or other and they wanted to be paid back. Hunter hated repaying favours or anything else, but sometimes his creditors insisted, and when that happened the only thing to do was sit and look sympathetic.

"They're so naive," said Hunter. "One of them even called me his buddy."

He says that last word as if he were holding it with a pair of tongs, thought Callan, and reached left-handed for his drink. When Hunter left Section headquarters he always took a minder with him, and if the minder didn't know his job he could wind up with a bullet in him while Hunter still moaned on about Americans so Callan drank his Scotch left-handed and sat between Hunter and the door of the pub, and watched and worried about every man and women who came in.

It was a nice pub: comfortable chairs, good Scotch, no canned music; but Callan hated it. He'd hate everything he had to do till Hunter was safely back in the Section H.Q. and he only had his own skin to worry about.

"Here he comes now," said Hunter, and Callan put his glass down and loosed the button of his coat. The man who came up to them wore a Madras cotton jacket of violent pattern, a brown straw hat, and three cameras. Callan could feel Hunter's dislike intensify. To Hunter all Americans were incredible, but American tourists were the most incredible of all—and a man who would actually choose to be an American tourist simply as a cover defied belief.

"Hi, Hunter old buddy," the American said.

If he goes on like this I'm going to have to kill him before Hunter does, Callan thought.

The American's gaze moved on from Hunter, and Callan noticed the man's eyes, grey and cold, with no depth in them at all. They looked like eyes made from very high-grade plastic. No tourist ever had eyes like that.

"Feeling nervous, son?" he asked.

80

"No," said Callan.

"Now you surprise me, you really do," the American said. "People who work with Hunter always end up nervous. I know I did."

"Please state your business," Hunter said.

"Well now," said the American. "That's a little difficult. I didn't realize you'd bring a witness along."

"I cannot leave headquarters without a bodyguard," said Hunter. "That's a rule."

"You mean you're got rules you actually keep?"

"Only my own," said Hunter.

The grey, shallow eyes looked even more blank than before.

Score one to Hunter, thought Callan.

"We've lost an operator," the American said.

"How very careless of you."

"And we'd kind of like him back."

"Who's got him?" Hunter asked.

"The K.G.B."

Hunter shrugged. "Then he's gone," he said. "Blown. Written off."

"That's a possibility, sure."

"With the K.G.B. it is much more than that."

"Not this time. The guy they picked up — Pete Merrick—he's been shot. I understand it's bad. Too bad for them to interrogate him. But he's got stuff they want. Their only hope is to get him out back to Russia, patch him up, and work on him there."

"Where is he now?" Hunter asked.

"We don't know for sure—but we think it's Southbay—on the Kent coast."

"You mounted an operation against the K.G.B. in Kent?" said Hunter.

"I guess we forgot to ask your permission."

Score one for the American, thought Callan.

"You were after a defector," Hunter said.

"Never mind what I was after."

"But I do mind. You were after Kholkov, and you started a blasted gun battle to get him—which you lost. And now you want me to rescue your gunman."

"I didn't want to—but I have to. I've only got one good man I can use here." He waited, but Hunter said nothing.

At last the American said: "You owe me this one."

"Very well," said Hunter. "But if I undertake to rescue this man Merrick for you—my debt is paid."

"O.K.," the American said. "I'll buy it. I have to."

He looked at Callan.

"Will he be on this?"

"Perhaps," said Hunter.

"Has he got a name?"

"Of course," said Hunter. "So have you. But I shan't introduce you. Both of you are already overburdened with secrets as it is. Give me the details, please."

That took twenty minutes of questioning, but in the end Hunter knew enough to make up his mind.

"We'll do what we can," he said. "But I can hardly promise to get Merrick back to you alive."

"So long as the Ivans don't get him," the American said, and Hunter smiled.

"That I can guarantee. Oh, by the way, you can stop looking for that defector Kholkov. I had him picked up this morning."

Game, set and match to Hunter, thought Callan. Now let's get him back inside H.Q.

The only lead to Merrick was the one good man the American had mentioned. His name was Hal Foder, and Callan had only needed to look at him once to know that he was deadly. When Hunter had announced that he wanted Foder as part of the team the American's eyes had looked blanker than ever, but in the end he'd agreed. The knowledge in Merrick's head was far more important than any agent's life.

Callan looked at Foder as they sat in a hamburger bar. Foder was cutting his food into infinitesimal pieces that he made no attempt to eat. The movements of his hands were neat and sure: long fingers, strong wrists, the hands of a gunman; and the top gunman's arrogance etched into the handsome face. Foder *knew* that nobody in the world was as good as he was. He would know it till the final bullet hit him, thought Callan, and by that time I could be dead too.

Foder said: "There were three of them. They hijacked our car on a back road near Folkestone. Merrick got out and started shooting. I guess they thought he was Kholkov."

"And you?"

"I was driving the car. I saw Merrick fall and then I crashed on through."

"You saw him hit?"

Foder nodded.

"Where?"

"Through the body. Twice."

"He could be dead."

"I doubt it," said Foder. "If he'd bean dead they'd have gone for me—instead of looking after him." He waited, but Callan said nothing.

"Look," Foder said. "I left him to die, O.K.? If I hadn't—they'd have killed me too."

"Maybe they will anyway," said Callan.

Southbay was small, well-off, and nosey. The big houses on the cliffs and the little houses behind them, sheltering from the winter gales, contained the biggest load of gossips Callan had ever met. All you had to do was sit and listen and they'd tell you their life-story—and everybody else's. But they'd none of them heard of strangers in the town and there weren't any new members of the yacht club with its row of sleek cruisers, any one of which had the power to move outside territorial waters and rendezvous with a Russian trawler. But the club did have a staff shortage. Everyone was agreed on that.

Callan went back to London, and called on Lonely. It was time the little man had a breath of sea air...

"Washer-up, Mr Callan?" Lonely said.

"That's right. Fifteen quid a week and your grub. You should do all right in the bar, too."

"I don't like that sort of work," said Lonely.

"You don't like any sort of work," said Callan. "That's why I'm offering a bonus. Fifty quid if you have to stay a week—a hundred if you get what I want."

"Just what do you want, Mr Callan?" Lonely asked.

Callan told him, and Lonely listened, enthralled.

"Mr Callan, it's not smugglers, is it?" he asked.

He looked at Callan entranced as he said it. "We had to say a poem at school about smugglers. Barrels of brandy they carried on ponies, and lace and tobacco and that."

You forgot about the letters for a spy, thought Callan.

"Never mind about smugglers," he said. "This is a straight forward hijack."

The little man looked nervous, and Callan reached for his handkerchief.

"Oh blimey," he said. "No need to start stinking the place out. You won't be there when it happens."

"You promise, Mr Callan?" said Lonely.

Callan said: "Don't I always?"

Lonely telephoned each day using a different callbox each time. The weather was nice, but the sea was too cold for a paddle and the only thing happening at Southbay was the washing up at the yacht club and that looked like it was going to last for ever.

On the third day Callan went to see Hunter.

"I don't like it," he said. "It's lasting too long."

"No," said Hunter. "They're waiting for the trawler. It won't be off Southbay till tomorrow."

"Suppose Merrick isn't there?"

"He's there all right," said Hunter.

"The only information we've got is Foder's. He's got a strong hunch that he'd seen the hijack car they used in Southbay. But it's still a hunch."

"We have rather more than that," said Hunter. "We have Kholkov's information too."

"Kholkov knows where they are?"

"Indeed he does."

"Then they'll have scarpered. They'll know they're blown."

Hunter shook his head.

"Kholkov was a cipher-clerk, no more—and the K.G.B. took damn good care that he didn't know where their safe-houses were. But a good defector knows that every scrap of useful information he brings with him will make his future life a little bit sweeter, and Kholkov is a very good defector indeed. He made a note of every phone call his masters made or took in his presence, and one was a Southbay number: a telephone answering service."

Hunter looked at the file open in front of him. "Among its clients is a Dr Ernest Webb."

"A doctor," said Callan, "would be a big help."

"In what way?"

"It would explain how a badly wounded man could be kept in hiding without medical attention."

Hunter nodded. It was always agreeable to be reminded that Callan was rather more than a steady hand and a fast trigger-finger.

"It would help if the doctor was a member of the yacht club."

"He's been a member for fifteen years," said Hunter. "He owns a big boat—and he's an excellent seaman." He paused. "Foder will help you?"

"You could put it like that," said Callan.

"Naturally I will leave the details to you," said Hunter. "But I must give one instruction. Webb came here as a refugee from Vienna in 1952. His name in those days was Weber. It seems likely that in the whole of the time since then he has worked for the K.G.B."

Hunter folded up the file and handled it to Callan.

"Webb is no concern of the C.I.A.," said Hunter. "You will attend to him personally."

Callan noted without surprise that the cover of Webb's file was red.

"I got on to you as soon as I heard, Mr Callan," said Lonely.

"That's all right old son. Take it easy," said Callan.

"They said he would be leaving tonight," said Lonely, "but I only heard the waiter talking about it this lunchtime." He looked nervously at Callan. "It only gives you an hour," he said.

Foder said, "It's damn close in here," and wound down the car window.

"Just relax," said Callan. "An hour's all we need."

"This Dr Webb's taking two of his mates on a trip," said Lonely.

"That's fine," said Callan.

"And one of them's a hell of a boozer."

"How do you know?" Callan asked.

"This doctor said the way he was going on he'd have to be carried on to the boat."

Callan made no answer, and Lonely looked up anxiously. "Is that all right, Mr Callan?" he asked.

Callan said: "That's just beautiful." He felt in his pocket and handed over 20 five-pound notes.

"Ta, Mr Callan," Lonely said. "You won't mind if I leave now, will you? If I hurry I'll just catch the last bus." He scrambled out, and Foder said: "Nothing like sea air for getting rid of a fug."

"Yeah," said Callan. "You sure you can handle a boat?"

"I'm sure," said Foder.

He still knows that nobody in the world's as good as he is, thought Callan. I hope to God he's wrong....

The boat was waiting for them in a deserted cove. Where Hunter had got it from or who had brought it, Callan had no idea, and far too much sense to ask. It was big and beamy, with a whacking great diesel that pushed it through the water like a giant hand shoving from behind. They got their feet wet scrambling into an inflatable dinghy to row out to her, and when they went aboard she smelled violently of fish.

And they say an agent's life is glamorous, thought Callan.

There was a pile of nets in the stern and Callan moved to sit on it, then thought better of it. For this kind of job you were safer on your feet.

The engine fired first time, and Foder took her out at half speed. As always his hands were deft and sure, and the boat responded easily. To the east of them, Southbay became a string of lights against the night sky, as the boat felt its way towards the darkness of the sea. As they eased their way forward, clouds parted, and a thin silver of moon showed, coaxing a glitter from the gun in Foder's hand. On reflex, Callan drew his Magnum .38 and instantly felt better.

"That damn moon's going to louse us up," said Foder. "Your Met. guys said ten-tenths cloud."

The boat moved on past the yacht harbour, and Callan could see a flurry of activity by one big sea-going cruiser. Foder put their boat out to sea, then eased back the engine. In the silence they could hear the muted roar of the cruiser starting up. As she moved from her moorings, cloud covered the moon.

"Actually we're rather proud of our Met. chaps." said Callan, then reached down and found the grappling hook Hunter had said would be there. Hunter thought of everything.

Foder doused the riding lights, and they waited in the darkness until suddenly the cruiser seemed to be coming straight at them. Foder swung their own boat and Callan threw the grappling hook as the two craft slammed into each other. Lonely would love this one, thought Callan. First it's smugglers, now it's ruddy pirates.

He leaped aboard the other boat and dropped flat on the deck. In the bows a large man was swearing in Russian and slipping the safety-catch of a Makavov automatic. Callan shot him and the gun continued in an unbroken sweep to cover the steersman. Webb looked at it, and his hands were already beginning to rise as Foder shot him dead.

Another red file closed, thought Callan. It's nice to think I didn't close it for once — and what Hunter doesn't know won't hurt him. He opened the cabin door and looked in. A man lay down there on a stretcher. A man who made no move at all.

"I'll need help," said Callan.

Between them Foder and he took Merrick aboard their own boat, and left Webb's cruiser to the dead. Callan bent to take Merrick's pulse, and behind him Foder said. "I'm sorry to have to do this." Callan looked back, into the mouth of Foder's gun.

"Merrick's going back to my boss, not to yours," Foder said. "And I don't want witnesses. I'm sorry."

He brought the gun up, and behind him the pile of nets stirred, flame seared the darkness and Foder fell.

"I'm sorry too," said Callan.

Meres wriggled out of the nets. "I stink of fish," he said, but Callan still stared down at Foder's body.

"What now?" said Meres.

"We put him on Webb's boat and start a fire," said Callan. He bent to pick up Foder. "I bet he still thinks he's the best," he said.

The big diesel chonked its way back to the deserted cove, and Callan looked out to sea where riding-lights gleamed. That would be the trawler, he thought. It'll have a good view of the fire. Suddenly behind them there came the dull whoosh of diesel oil bursting into red, dirty flame. In its light Meres looked down at Merrick.

"What happens to him?" he asked.

"Foder was wrong," said Callan. "Merrick goes to our boss after all. He knows things Hunter wants to know, poor bastard."

File on a Man Called Callan

"THIS one you will treat with the utmost seriousness," said Hunter.

You could never be sure, but Callan had a feeling that, deep down inside himself where no one could see, Hunter was laughing. He looked at the file that Hunter held. White cover: surveillance only. Where was the utmost seriousness in that? Hunter passed the file to him across the desk.

"Take a look at it," he said. "I think you will appreciate what I mean."

Callan turned the cover to find he was looking at a photograph of himself.

"You've got me under surveillance?" he asked.

This time Hunter smiled: an indulgence he permitted himself perhaps five times a year.

"Toby Meres will be keeping an eye on you," he said.

"What on earth am I supposed to have done?" Callan asked.

"That is not the question," said Hunter. "It's more a matter of what you're going to do."

When he's whimsical he's murder, thought Callan. Aloud he said, "What am I going to do then—sir?"

Hunter's smile vanished. "Kill somebody," he said.

"Anybody I know?" said Callan.

"Not even anybody I know," said Hunter. "I had a signal from our chap in Moscow the other day. The K.G.B. are very angry about Lubov's defection.

"They would be," said Callan. "Lubov's the best one we've ever got."

Hunter looked smug. "A full colonel in military Intelligence," he said, "the highest ranking agent ever to come over." The smugness vanished. "The K.G.B. want to kill him."

"They'll have to find him first," said Callan.

"They think they can find him," said Hunter. "Or rather they've been approached by a couple of freelancers who've offered to do the job for them."

"A contract?"

"One hundred thousand pounds on the day he dies."

Callan whistled. This was big money.

"Moreover," Hunter said, "they knew where Lubov was going."

This was a bad one. When Hunter called a place a safe-house it was exactly that: safe. It had to be—or defectors like Lubov wouldn't do business ever again.

"I want you to kill whoever's been given the job of killing Lubov," said Hunter. He paused. "Lubov was going to Westlake. Do you know it?"

Callan shook his head.

"It's a rest home and health resort kind of place in Surrey." Hunter said. "You'll detest it. Alcohol is forbidden."

Callan shrugged. He could live with that. The only time he needed a drink was after a job. "What's my cover?" he said.

"You're Lubov," said Hunter.

"Come off it," said Callan. "My Russian's terrible."

"Lubov's English is excellent," said Hunter. "He even has a cockney accent."

"But they'll *know* I'm not him."

"He is very similar in build to you," said Hunter. "And we have, of course, given him plastic surgery. His face is bandaged. I shall make it possible for the K.G.B. to find that out."

"I see," said Callan. "Is Toby going with me?"

"Toby is there already. Don't look so worried, David. He's an excellent bodyguard."

"Yeah," said Callan. "And I'm an excellent target."

He went through the rest of the file then. Large-scale map of Westlake and the surrounding countryside: personnel; guests; a list of possible freelancers who'd taken on the contract.

Westlake itself looked marvelous; an eighteenth-century manor house in seven acres of grounds; landscape gardens, lake and trees; the lot. The personnel seemed all right too. Resident doctor, couple of nurses — good-looking birds the pair of them—maids, masseurs, waiters. The list of possible freelancers which Hunter handed to Callan wasn't so good. Hunter looked at Callan's face and said: "Something wrong?"

"None of the freelancers on this list is up to this job," Callan said.

"I agree with you," said Hunter. "I'm afraid it does make it rather more difficult."

"It might also make me dead," said Callan.

"Ah yes. That reminds me—are you thinking of using your odoriferous little friend on this one?"

"He'd be useful," said Callan.

"He'll be in enormous danger."

"So will Toby," said Callan. "So will I."

"But there is a difference," said Hunter. "You and Toby are aware of the danger. Lonely isn't."

"I could give him a hint."

"No," said Hunter. "If Lonely panics you could be blown. Let him stay ignorant. It's his natural state, after all. That's an order, Callan."

"Very good—sir," said Callan.

Lonely sucked at his pint as Callan talked. "Sounds dead easy," he said at last.

"Dead easy," said Callan. "Yeah."

He looked at the little man. Fear and dependency struggling inside a body that had never known how to fight back; only to suffer. ... Dead. ... Easy.

"The only thing is," said Lonely, "I don't like the country."

"Blimey, what's wrong with it?" said Callan. "Good food. Fresh air. Do you the world of good."

"It's all empty," said Lonely. "I'm nervous when there's no people about. Always have been ever since I was evacuated. Big git of a farmer. Used to belt me 'cos I niffed."

All his life, thought Callan. All his miserable, bloody life. He watched again as Lonely dived back into, his pint ... Dead ... So very easy.

"All right, old son," he said. "I won't push you on this one."

Lonely looked up at him. Something in Callan's voice was wrong. He was worried about something. Worried bad.

"Is this one dangerous, Mr Callan?" he asked.

"No," said Callan. "I'm going to see a bird in this place, that's all. And I'm bothered her husband might come looking. I just want to find out if he's there or not."

"Well if that's all," said Lonely. "I don't see why I couldn't oblige you. I mean it's only a couple of nights, innit? And a hundred quid would come in handy."

"But you don't like the country," said Callan.

In the end Lonely had to talk him into letting him go.

Callan went to Westlake in a Rolls with dark-tinted windows, his forehead, nose, and cheeks covered with adhesive bandage. The man who drove him had once won a Monte Carlo Rally, the two men who sat on either side of him were Section trained—and deadly: beneath his coat he could feel the hard comfort of a Magnum .38 and yet he was afraid. To become a target is to know nothing but fear. It dominates even your dreams....

As the great car swept along a gravel path between smooth-shaven lawns he saw the beauty of the house in its bower of trees, but the beauty had no meaning. Every room in the house could conceal an assassin, every tree hide a sniper. The two bodyguards flanked him as he walked quickly into the house, the chauffeur three steps behind carrying Callan's case.

Up a stairway carpeted in deep pile to a room with soft-leather chairs and an antique sofa-table. The way the rich lived—or died.

He crossed to the window of bullet-proof glass and watched the bodyguards get back into the Rolls and leave. He watched, but heard nothing. The bullet-proof glass was so thick it completely sound-proofed the room.

"You'll have Toby after all," Hunter had said. "That should be enough. David. We want to make it difficult for them to get at you. I agree — but not impossible. If we make it impossible, they might not bother to try."

Callan thought: "That would suit me fine."

Behind him a woman's voice said, "Good evening, Mr Smith."

The gun was in Callan's hands before he'd finished turning....

89

A nurse. A pretty one. Dark, coiled hair, and a luscious mouth at odds with the uniform's austerity. She looked at the Magnum without fear, almost without surprise. She had seen scores of guns—and scores of nervous Mr Smiths. Callan put the Magnum away.

"I'm sorry," he said. "Sister Johnson, isn't it?"

"Sister Lynn," said the nurse.

"I was told I'd have Sister Johnson."

"Johnson's got a bit of a tummy upset,' said Sister Lynn. "I'm taking her place."

Callan felt the first cold breath of panic. Something was wrong. The nurse looked at his face.

"I assure you I'm perfectly efficient," she said.

Lonely humped his suitcase to the twenty-seventh door. Not a bad dodge this going on the knocker, especially when the sun was shining. Mind you, the case got heavy after a bit, but there was a nice little pub down the road where you could set it down and rest your legs. He pressed the door-bell and opened the case.

"Good evening, sir," he said. "I wonder if I could interest you in this really excellent little transistor radio." He pressed a button, and number three in the top twenty belted out in the prospect's face.

"Only seven pound fifty, sir, and—"

"Get lost," said the prospect, and slammed the door.

And up yours too, mate thought Lonely. I bet you didn't know you just had your picture taken. He adjusted the tiny camera inside the radio, made a note of the house-number, and approached door number 28. Twenty-five houses, two caravans, and a tent. All houses of new arrivals—or strangers. It had cost him a mint in beer money to find out, but that went on expenses. He was still a hundred quid ahead—and he'd sold three transistor radios that hadn't cost him anything in the first place. Lonely thought he might get to like the country after all.

Meres looked at the windows of toughened glass, windows he would never dare to open.

"Do you mind if we have the air-conditioning on? It's getting rather close in here," he said.

"Yeah," said Callan. "I do mind. The noise puts me off."

"You are an old worry-guts, aren't you?" said Meres. "Just because a nurse has a tummy upset."

"According to the file it's the first time she's been ill since she came here," said Callan. "It's too much of a coincidence that it happens when I arrive."

Meres sighed. Callan was marvelous at his job and all that, but he did worry so, "I checked with the doctor," he said. "He treated her himself."

But Callan went on worrying. "Why do I have to have a nurse, anyway? I'm not ill," he said.

"Cover, old boy. You've had an operation—or you would have done if you'd been Lubov. So you have to have a nurse."

Callan looked at his watch.

"Time you checked with Lonely," he said.

"I don't like leaving you," said Meres.

"Don't get me wrong, Toby," Callan said, "but your leaving me is the best chance I've got."

Meres climbed into the passenger seat of Lonely's car, and sniffed, but Lonely smelled only of fish and chips and beer. Things must be going well, though Meres, and took the rolls of film and tatty notebook Lonely gave him.

"That's the lot," said Lonely. "Every single one that's been here under a year."

"You have been busy," said Meres.

"My bleeding plates is on fire," said Lonely. "And all because of a bird."

"What bird?" said Meres.

The smooth, educated voice was as soft as ever, but there was death in it, and Lonely knew it. The smell came then.

"Mr Callan's bird," said Lonely. "The one with the husband."

"Oh, that bird," said Meres. "Have you talked about her—in the village?"

"Of course not," said Lonely. "Mr Callan said to keep shtum."

"Keep very shtum indeed," said Meres. "Otherwise I might just have to pay you a little visit."

Callan had set up a dark corner in the bathroom and together they developed the negatives and went through the notes. The pile of photographs was reduced to three and then to one.

"I think so," said Meres.

"I bloody know so," said Callan. He picked up the phone and dialled the old, familiar number.

"Let me speak to Charlie, please," he said.

They put him through, and he talked, and Hunter listened.

"Yes," Hunter said at last. "She has. An identical twin. Was in the diplomatic service. Resigned for what are called private reasons. That could mean dishonesty."

"Where was his last posting?" Callan asked.

The silence that followed was worse than a scream.

Hunter said, "Moscow. He had excellent opportunities to make K.G.B. contacts. And he has a hobby, David—one he's very good at. Pistol shooting. He's in the Olympic class."

"That's all I needed," said Callan. He hung up and turned to Meres. "Stay with her," he said. "Don't leave her."

"What about you, old boy?" said Meres.

Callan said: "I'm about to find out if I'm in the Olympic class too."

*

The morning was clear and still. Callan looked out at the gleaming green of the grass, the white puff balls of cloud that heightened the blueness of the sky. Sunlight and shady trees and a boat already moving on the lake. A day when it should be good to be alive. He went to the shower, and took the Magnum with him then came back in his dressing-gown and lay on the bed.

Sister Lynn bustled into the room, with coffee, eggs and toast on a tray and but it on the bed.

"How's Sister Johnson this morning?" he asked.

"Much better," said the nurse. "She'll be back on duty before lunch."

So it's going to be soon, though: Callan. Toby, old son, don't go to sleep on me.

"That's nice," he said, and smiled. Despite the criss-cross of bandages, it was a very expressive smile.

"But I'll miss you," he said, and as he said it the warning came. Something was wrong.

"Just listen to the birds," said Sister Lynn, and Callan erupted from the bed, coffee sprayed the covers, and Sister Lynn felt herself pushed to the ground under Callan's weight as a bullet slapped into the depression in the pillow his head had made.

"But it can't—" she said.

"It can if you open the window and hear the birds sing," said Callan.

"I didn't. I promise you I didn't," she said, but he crawled across the room in a fury of speed and another bullet slammed into the floor inches from his head before he reached the security of the wall by the window. Slowly he raised himself and looked down. The man was using a tree for cover. Trees always were dodgy. You could see his leg.

Callan moved from cover, fired and ducked down, and the man stumbled then hobbled to the window in a shambling run and fired again. The bullet whisked the cap from Sister Lynn's head. Callan fired, and the man pitched forward in mid-stride. This time he didn't get up.

"I didn't," Sister Lynn said, and the luscious mouth trembled. "Honestly I didn't."

"No love," said Callan. "Not you."

He raced to the nurses' room down the hall and found Meres holding a gun on Sister Johnson.

Meres said: "She went to the loo. I didn't take my eyes off her for two minutes."

"It only takes seconds to open a window," said Callan.

"I really am sorry, David."

"Never mind," said Callan. "At least I know I could win a medal."

"I haven't the remotest idea what you're talking about," said Sister Johnson.

"We're talking about the fact that my friend here just killed your twin brother," said Meres.

Calmly, without haste, she picked up her handbag.

"No," said Callan, and snatched it from her. Inside the bag was a Beretta automatic and a phial of pills. Callan held on to the gun and put the pills in his dressing-gown pocket.

"Are they what gave you the collywobbles?" he asked.

She made no answer.

"Why did you do it, love? To give yourself an alibi and put the blame on Sister Lynn for opening the window?"

"My brother," she said. "You killed my brother." The voice held first amazement, then screaming rage, and her hands reached for Callan like claws, but Meres tripped her and she fell, still screaming, until Meres said softly. "Perhaps you think I wouldn't ill treat a woman. I'd be happy to show you how wrong you are."

The screaming stopped then, and she said, "I hate you. My brother's dead and I hate you."

"If I were you I'd save your voice," said Meres. "You've got to talk to Charlie, and he can listen for hours."

Callan walked back to his room. Sister Lynn was still there, trying to clear up the wreckage of his breakfast, her white uniform splashed with coffee, her hair askew. She rose as he entered.

"Forgive the cliché," she said, "but I think you saved my life."

"It's a life worth saving," said Callan. He looked down at his hands. No shakes. Not this time.

"Is anything wrong?" she asked.

Callan said: "I know it's early, but for some reason I want a drink—and this place is dry."

"Only for patients," she said. "Staff have certain privileges."

"Like whisky?"

"I do happen to have a bottle in my room," she said. "If we could sneak in without anyone seeing us—."

"Just a minute," said Callan, and tugged at the bandages on his face.

"Let me," she said, and he felt the smooth strength of her fingers till the last one fell away, and she stood very close, looking at his face.

"I knew you had a nice smile," she said, and kissed him.

Later Callan said: "You mentioned whisky."

"In my room," she said. "But only for staff."

"Look love," said Callan, "when it comes to nurses and whisky, believe me—I'm staff too."

File on a Gallic Charmer

CALLAN waited in silence as Hunter stacked the three yellow-backed flies neatly together, then handed them to him.

"Three at once," said Callan. "You're spoiling me."

"That isn't my intention," Hunter said, then hesitated.

Blimey, what's this? Callan wondered. He's actually embarrassed.

Hunter said at last: "Has it ever occurred to you what a damn nuisance sex can be?"

"Never," said Callan.

"What I've just given you is the eternal triangle," said Hunter. "God knows I hate clichés—but it's the only way to describe it."

Callan flicked through the flies: Professor Harvey Everitt, M.A., Ph.D., D.Sc., Mrs Jane Everitt, and Marcel Christophe: a plain man, a pretty woman, and a Gallic charmer.

"Everitt's field is electronics," said Hunter. "He's currently working on a tracking device for ballistic missiles. I understand it's the best of its kind."

"Has he got naughty friends then?" Callan asked.

"No. He's quite secure. Nothing in his background—never even visited Russia. He's all right. It's that blasted wife of his."

He really is uptight about this one, thought Callan.

"She's bored," Hunter said. "Bored with her husband, bored with her life. No children and a more than adequate income. Women like that are always ripe for mischief."

"So she falls for Marcel," said Callan.

"Precisely," said Hunter.

"And what does Marcel do for a living?" Callan asked.

Hunter said. "He's a chef."

"With respect sir," said Callan, "even you have to be joking this time."

"No damn it, I'm not." said Hunter. "He runs a cordon-bleu school and that blasted woman's his star pupil."

"Does the professor know?"

"He suspects," Hunter said. "And it's affecting his work."

Callan said: "Are you sure this is my kind of job, sir?"

"Of course," said Hunter "Why do you ask?"

"It sounds more like advice to the love-lorn," said Callan.

Suddenly Hunter's embarrassment vanished. "If it is, you're going to be Aunt Mabel who writes the column," he said.

He's made his mind up, Callan thought. So where's the point in fighting?

"Exactly what am I supposed to do?" he asked.

"Observe them," Hunter said. "If Christophe is what he purports to be—and no more—then persuade him to transfer his affections somewhere else. I'll leave the details to you."

"I thought you would," said Callan. "Suppose he's more than he purports to be?"

"Then we'll give him a red file," said Hunter. "And I'll still leave the details to you."

L'Ecole de la Cuisine Francaise was on the third floor of a well-preserved Georgian house in a well-preserved Georgian Square. Callan sat in a car and watched them come and go, women for the most part, but with the odd man among them as well—and all well-heeled by the look of them—talking of roux and marmites and béchamel sauce.

"I can't go in and sign on with this lot," Callan thought. "I can't even fry chips. They'd be on to me in a minute."

He watched Jane Everitt arrive, and run lightly up the steps to the house. She was even prettier than her photograph, and the look on her face had nothing to do with cooking. Slowly, reluctantly, Callan got out of the car. As always, Hunter was right. There were times when sex was a damn nuisance.

*

The first thing you noticed about the place was the smell. Even before you opened the door it was there to greet you: a rich, delicious blend of fine meat roasting, of salmon poaching in champagne, of pheasant and hare and asparagus and fruit. Callan knocked on the door and went inside.

The whole place seemed to be one enormous kitchen. Everywhere dedicated men and women in butchers' aprons were doing wonderful things with meat, with fish, with game. The smell was more delicious than ever.

Callan looked around: no sign of Christophe—or of Jane Everitt. He went up to a man in a pin-striped suit who was lining a bowl with alternating rows of peas, turnip, French beans, and carrot strips.

"I'm making a partridge chartreuse," the man said.

"Pretty," said Callan. "Where— ?"

"Tricky too."

"I'm sure," said Callan. "Where's M. Christophe?"

"In his office. Over there."

The man gesture vaguely, never taking his eyes from his work. He might have been Leonardo working on the Mona Lisa.

Callan knocked on the door and went in at once. Jane Everitt and Christophe were standing very close together, and she still had that look in her eyes that had nothing to do with cooking. Christophe wore the full chef's rig: tall hat, white apron, but he didn't look as if his thoughts were on cooking either.

95

"I beg your pardon," said Callan. "My wife asked me to look in. She's thinking of enrolling."

The woman scowled at him, but Christophe turned to Callan with the weary efficiency of a man who has told the same story five hundred times before.

Callan was shown the kitchen, its equipment, its pupils, its achievement, and given brochures that dealt with everything from fees to hours of attendance, and then, very firmly but very politely, he was shown the door. And all the time, Callan noticed, the men and women watched Christophe as pupils watch a master. He mightn't have been the greatest cook in the world, but they seemed to think he was, and by the look of them, they'd be good judges. But was there more to him than a tall, white hat?

Whether he was a spy or not is was impossible to tell. But there was a strong chance he might be bent. Rich, bored women were sitting ducks for blackmail and Hunter would want to know about that too. Callan decided to take expert opinion. As a gourmet Lonely was a disaster, but when it came to nosing out a crook he was on his own.

"I don't go for that foreign muck, Mr Callan," Lonely said. "Frogs' legs and snails and that. You'd wonder how people could bring themselves to swallow it."

"I'm not asking you to have dinner with him," said Callan. "I only want you to have a look at him."

"What for, Mr Callan?"

"Five quid," said Callan.

Lonely said: "You're on."

They had to wait till school came out, then star pupil and teacher appeared at last, and walked to a pub nearby and Lonely followed. Callan waited in another pub, across the street. They'd seen him once: it would have been foolish to push his luck again so soon. He sipped one cautious Scotch and waited till Christophe and Jane Everitt walked back down the street, and Lonely came in and waited while Callan bought beer.

"Funny feller, Mr Callan," Lonely said. "He bought a bottle of wine."

"What's funny about that?" said Callan.

"He's going to cook with it. You ask me—all foreigners is barmy."

"All I'm asking you is—is he bent?"

Lonely sucked at his pint and considered, and Callan waited, willing himself to patience. There was no point in fussing the little man. His instincts had always worked a damn sight faster than his brains.

"A bit difficult that one," Lonely said at last. "He's been in the nick all right—I could tell the way he smoked his fag—but whether he's bent now or not..." He shrugged. "I tell you one thing, Mr Callan, he's potty about that bird. Maybe she's on to him to go straight. Birds do that."

"That the best you can do?" Callan asked.

"Well I didn't have much of a chance now, did I?" said Lonely. Callan gave him a fiver.

"Is a bird on to you to go straight?" he asked.

"That'll be the day," said Lonely.

"In that case," said Callan, "you and me will pull a job."

But for that they had to wait till the school was empty, and that night it wasn't. Marcel cooked dinner, and he and Jane spent an awfully long time eating it, while Callan kept a watch on the house and sent Lonely for fish and chips.

Then Jane left on her own, and Callan followed her out to the neat suburb where she and the professor lived, and on to a pub where she joined her husband, and Callan watched and listened discreetly.

The professor already had a woman with him when Jane arrived, and it was clear from the Arctic politeness each woman used to the other that they hated each other intensely. Dr Cobb, Jane called her. Laura Cobb, M.A., Ph.D.

The files said she was Everitt's research assistant, and that she was brilliant. They didn't mention that she was a disaster to look at: hair in a mess, laddered tights, face and hands grubby. She could have been quite pretty, if someone had taken the trouble to clean her up, but it didn't look as though anyone had ever bothered.

She and Everitt were eating the kind of standard pub food that Christophe wouldn't have fed to his cat, and by the look of them they were enjoying it. As they ate they talked the kind of scientific jargon that is sheer gibberish to anyone outside the club, and Jane sat and listened and looked bored. Callan glanced at the pub mirror, and found that he looked bored too.

"I've had a little more information from Everitt's security people," said Hunter. "Nice of them, considering they handed the whole mess over to me in the first place. It seems that Christophe's French all right, so far as his passport goes, and he's a damn good chef. He must be. Used to run a restaurant near Lyons that had two rosettes in Michelin. But he's only been over here three months and nobody knows where he got the money to start that school. It cost is him a packet to do it, too. I don't like it, David. Mrs Everitt's been keen on this cuisine business for years. It all fits too neatly."

"What do you think he's going to try?" Callan asked. "Kidnapping her?"

"It's possible," said Hunter. "You know it's possible. We've worked the same trick ourselves. And he went to Air France the other day about flights to Paris."

"He bothers me," said Callan. "He doesn't look like a pro—not our kind of pro. Can you find out if he's ever been to prison?"

"Why do you ask?"

"Just a feeling somebody had."

Hunter made a note.

"It may take a day or two," he said. "In the meantime I want you to stay with him. Everitt is very important indeed, and his work's almost finished.

"That must be a nice feeling," said Callan.

"Except that his emotional life's in such tangle he's incapable of finishing it," said Hunter. "Get back to Christophe, David. I want to know what he's up to."

They got their chance the next night, when Christophe and Jane went to the cinema together. It was a treat to watch Lonely practice his craft. When nothing was worrying him and he had Callan for a minder he could do a real virtuoso's job. They couldn't have got in more easily if Christophe had loaned them his keys.

Once inside they began their search. Apart from the enormous kitchen, the place was simply an office, a bedroom and a sitting room, all furnished by the yard; comfortable, expensive, and totally anonymous. No photographs, no personal letters. The only mark of a personality in the whole place was a collection of cookery books.

Patiently Callan sat down to go through the drawers of Christophe's office desk, and Lonely wandered off, yawning. He'd been told not to pinch anything, and anyway, there was nothing worth pinching.

Half an hour later, Callan decided that it was time to go. He looked around for Lonely, and found him in the kitchen. It seemed that the little man had got over his objection to French cooking. When Callan entered the room he'd already finished off a cup of cold consommé and a slice of Ardennes paté, and was halfway through a duck á l'orange, which he appeared to be going to wash down with a Clos de Vougeot '61, bottled *en domaine*.

"Aren't you going to keep a bit for me?" Callan asked.

Lonely waved a lordly hand.

"Help yourself, Mr Callan," he said.

"You great nit," said Callan. "He wasn't supposed to know we've been here."

Suddenly the place smelled of rather more than food.

"But Mr Callan," Lonely said, "with all this food around he wouldn't miss one little tiny bit."

"Tiny bit? You've got a whole bloody duck there," said Callan. "Sure you didn't fancy the partridge-chartreuse as well?"

"The what, Mr Callan?"

Callan pointed at the bowl on which the pinstripe suited man had worked so hard.

"Oh that," said Lonely. "I tried that. Didn't fancy it, Soggy," he explained.

Callan sighed.

"Come on," he said.

"We leaving, Mr Callan?"

"Not yet we're not," said Callan. "You've got to do the washing up."

After that they let themselves out, Lonely scarpered, and Callan went out to the suburbs to look at Everitt. Might as well, he thought. There's nothing to report on Christophe, and Hunter hates it when there's nothing to report....

The house was quiet, and to a pupil of Lonely's the lock was a joke. Callan let himself in, and three minutes later he let himself out again.

He knew, while he was there, that he was not alone in the house.

He could hear the faintest of sounds coming from a bedroom. There were two people there. But, it seemed, they were occupied.

Callan left, making no more noise than snowflakes falling.

Suddenly, for no reason he could explain, didn't want to explain, the alarm bell started bonging in his head and he looked back towards the house.

Dr Cobb was standing at the window looking down at him. Her negligée was grubby. She had no reason to be there. Callan had never seen so much venom concentrated in one face.

He drove back to headquarters quickly. For this one he would need a woman, and Hunter's secretary was certainly that—and much, much more.

"But I can't," said Liz.

"Of course you can," said Callan.

"But she'll know it's the wrong voice."

"I went to the lab to see George," said Callan. "He loaned me this." As he spoke his fingers screwed a neat plastic cylinder to the mouthpiece of the telephone.

"This'll make it sound like a bad line," he said, and passed Liz the phone.

"Now remember," he said. "Your husband's leaving you for this bitch and you don't give a damn. In fact, as soon as you're hung up, you're on your way to your boy friend to celebrate."

"She'll tell Everitt," said Liz.

"She can't," said Callan. "Everitt's due at a War Office conference in 10 minutes. Even she can't reach him there."

Liz took the phone and dialled the number of Everitt's research establishment.

"Dr Laura Cobb, please ... This is Mrs Everitt."

The voice was cool—the boss's wife's voice—but there was amusement in it, too.

She waited, then said. "Laura, darling. I bet I didn't even give you time to take your coat off. ... Yes, it is a bad line, isn't it? ... I didn't recognise you either. Listen ... it's about our darling husband."

Callan marvelled at what bitches even the nicest women can be and Liz finished at last and hung up.

"Was it all right?" she asked.

"I think you're done that before," said Callan. "It was great."

"Suppose she just runs away?" Liz asked.

"She won't," Callan said. "Toby Meres is watching her—and women don't run away from Toby. Not when he's got a gun in his hand."

"You think she'll go to the chef's place?"

"I think somebody will," said Callan.

He set off for Christophe's at once, but traffic was bad, and Dr Cobb hadn't wasted any time.

From outside the door he could hear Jane Everitt's voice saying. "I haven't the remotest idea what you're talking about."

"Please don't lie," a man's voice said. "You accused Dr Cobb of planning to run away with your husband to Russia and we want to know how you came by your suspicions."

"Who's we?" Christophe asked.

"Security," said the voice.

Callan had only heard that voice once before. But he recognised it. The man in the pin-stripe still. The man who had been making partridge chartreuse.

Security is right, Callan thought, but you didn't say whose mate.

He drew back his foot for the karate kick that had to break the door-lock. If it didn't, he would be dead. Then his leg straightened in a flash of speed, the lock shattered and his shoulder hit the door blasting it open.

He fell prone behind a gas-cooker and the man in the pin-stripe suit whirled and fired.

Callan fired too, as a Makarov bullet gouged into a copper-bottomed pan and ricocheted past his head. The man in the pin-stripe suit had a hole in his forehead. It grew wider, and Jane Everitt opened her mouth to scream, but no sound came.

*

"The Reds recruited Cobb when she was at university," said Hunter. "She kept very quiet about it. Never told a soul."

"She talked to you," said Callan.

Hunter said: "They all do, sooner or later." Callan felt cold.

"Now," said Hunter. "What about Christophe?"

"He's a chef," said Callan, "and that's all he is."

"But he went to prison," Hunter said. "You were right about that. He did six months in France for assault."

"On another chef," said Callan. "For insulting a sauce he invented."

"All the same," said Hunter, "he did open that school — and I don't like coincidences."

"There aren't any," said Callan. "Jane Everitt met him at that restaurant he ran near Lyons. She was on what they call a gastronomic tour. He came over here and opened the school so that they could be together."

"But where the devil did he get the money?"

"He didn't want to tell me that—but I knew anyway. It was in his bank book. He invented a new sauce for baked beans."

Hunter glared at him.

"I'm in no mood for jokes, Callan," he said.

"This is deadly serious," said Callan. "A canning company paid him a fortune for it."

"Then why keep it a secret?" Hunter asked.

"Because he's a master chef," said Callan. "It's like Shakespeare doing cracker mottoes."

"I suppose it is," said Hunter, and very nearly smiled.

"Bit of luck you getting their hatchet man," he said.

"No sir," said Callan. "I was on to him anyway."

Hunter said: "Nonsense. How could you possibly be?"

"Because he was a lousy cook," said Callan. "Even Lonely spotted that."

The Scripts

Goodness Burns Too Bright

by

James Mitchell

Editor's Introduction

Even as the one-off television play which introduced the enigmatic agent David Callan, *A Magnum for Schneider*, was broadcast in February 1967, plans were in hand for a regular series of Callan adventures under the guidance of author James Mitchell and associate producer Terence Feely. Early fans (which included Prime Minister Harold Wilson) did not have long to wait and the first series of six black-and-white episodes of *Callan* starring Edward Woodward in the title role was launched in July.

Sadly, none of that first series are known to exist today, the original recordings having been made on video-tape and subsequently wiped or lost, and no copies of James Mitchell's original scripts were found among his papers after his death in 2002.

In 2012, eagle-eyed long-time *Callan* fan Mandy Knighton-Clark spotted a number of early scripts for sale on eBay, including many of the 'missing' episodes from Series 1 in 1967 and Series 2, which began broadcast in January 1969. These were 'Camera Scripts' - technical shooting scripts, as used by ABC Television at their Teddington Lock studios in Middlesex, rather than the original 'dramatic' narrative scripts James Mitchell would have submitted. Among them was *Goodness Burns Too Bright*, Mitchell's first script for the television series after his original *A Magnum for Schneider*. It was recorded at Teddington Studios on the 18th and 19th April 1967 and broadcast as Episode 4 of Season 1 of *Callan* on the 29th July.

The 71-page shooting script is a script primarily for the use of the director and technical crew rather than the actors and contains precise camera and microphone directions relating to specific studio sets (virtually all the action of *Goodness Burns Too Bright* takes place 'indoors'), which often make it difficult for the general reader to follow the plot. Television scripts are, of course, designed to be filmed and *seen* rather than read and whilst there are technical commands for the cameramen (whether the actors move left or right across a set; whether they enter or leave; close-ups; which actor is 'favoured' in a group shot; where the camera should settle on a particular prop, and so on), there are virtually no indicators as to how the cast should *act* the piece. Such dramatic decisions would have been taken at cast read-throughs and rehearsals, but as no copy of the actual recording exists, it is sometimes difficult to work out from the shooting script what exactly is going on!

Some pages of the shooting script have clearly been replaced – last minute alterations which are often known as 'pink pages' because additional pages of script tended to be printed on pink paper. There are no clues (that I can see) as to why alterations were necessary or what was replaced.

In some instances – crucial ones – the technical directions are sparse. During Act 2, a scene with Callan and the villainous Bauer is labelled simply: "THEY FIGHT", yet what must have taken place would have been a specific, well-rehearsed piece of violence, the consequences of which are crucial to the plot and the action in Act 3. Yet without *seeing* how "They Fight" was acted out on screen, reading the script 'blind' as it were (without the images) is confusing to say the least.

In this instance – and in one or two other minor cases – I have taken the liberty of trying to suggest the *actions* of the actors as they perform James Mitchell's trademark short, sharp dialogue. In doing so, I have had to second-guess the instructions of the episode's director and the input of a cast of very experienced actors, as I never saw *Goodness Burns Too Bright* when it was broadcast. Any mistakes or misinterpretations are therefore entirely my fault, but I hope I have kept to the spirit of *Callan* in trying to make these pages more reader-friendly.

The basic changes I have made have been the removal of technical instructions concerning camera angles and the placement of microphones and the addition of 'stage directions' to indicate which characters are where and what they are doing. Apart from correcting typographical and spelling errors, the dialogue is exactly as written by James Mitchell and has not been changed or cut.

Goodness Burns Too Bright is set initially in London – with an all-too-brief cameo role for Callan's wonderful sidekick Lonely – but then moves to West Berlin, a divided city in 1967 and the epicentre of the Cold War. It is an unusual episode in that Callan's great rival in 'The Section', the upper-class bully Toby Meres (so wonderfully played by Anthony Valentine), does not appear but is replaced by the similarly untrustworthy 'Maitland'. I believe this to be Maitland's one and only appearance in the *Callan* canon (Maitland is integral to the plot because of his previous relationship with the German agent Bauer) and he was played by Jeremy Lloyd, who died in December 2014, at the time a jobbing actor but subsequently to become famous as the creator and writer of comedy shows such as *Are You Being Served?* and *'Allo 'Allo*.

Alone, hurt and on the run in Berlin, Callan benefits from the sympathetic treatment he receives (the goodness that 'burns too bright' of the title) at the hands of the widowed 'Dr Schultz' – a role taken by one of England's acting legends, Gladys Cooper, at the age of 79 in the year she was made a Dame.

As the editor of two volumes of Callan short stories, I have learned not to be surprised when previously-thought 'missing' Callan material turns up when least expected! It would not shock me at all to learn that someone, somewhere, had just discovered a fragile, 48-year-old video-tape of *Goodness Burns Too Bright* in a garage or an attic. Until that happens, I hope my reconstructed script can at least give a tiny flavour of one of the truly creations of British television drama.

Goodness Burns Too Bright

A *Callan* episode

Recorded at ABC Television's Teddington Lock Studios on 18th &19th April 1967.
    Broadcast as Episode 4 of Season 1 of *Callan* on 29th July 1967.
    No known copy of this recording exists.

CAST:

Callan	....	EDWARD WOODWARD
Hunter	....	RONALD RADD
Maitland	....	JEREMY LLOYD
Lonely	....	RUSSELL HUNTER
Eva	....	ROSEMARY FRANKAU
Bauer	....	ROBERT LANG
Franz	....	LESLIE WHITE
Dr Schultz	....	GLADYS COOPER

Associate Producer .... Terence Feely

Executive Producer .... Lloyd Shirley

Directed by .... Bill Bain

Note: INT. means the scene is an Interior setting (as opposed to EXT. or exterior) and **SOV.** means *Sound of Voice* only when an actor is off-screen or to illustrate thought rather than direct speech.

INT. SECTION HQ. DAY

> *Hunter and Maitland in Hunter's office*
> *watching close circuit TV monitors of*
> *the road outside. A car draws up.*

HUNTER:
(SOV)

There's the car now.

> *The CCTV camera zooms in and*
> *a figure emerges from the car.*

HUNTER:
(SOV)

That's Bauer.

> *They stand and move away from the monitors.*
> *Hunter indicates a chair in front of his desk.*

HUNTER:

We'll put him here. Light enough for you?

> *Maitland pulls a chair to behind the*
> *one indicated by Hunter.*

MAITLAND: Fine. I'd like to be here, sir, if you don't mind. With Bauer one always likes to be sure.

HUNTER: He's that good?

MAITLAND: He has to be. He's still alive. He's given us a lot of trouble in Berlin.

HUNTER: I know. That's why we brought you over.

MAITLAND: What's he after, sir?

HUNTER: He wants us to find him a victim.

MAITLAND: A lamb to the slaughter?

HUNTER: Precisely. And we are going to supply the lamb.

> *Close up on Maitland gently touching*
> *the gun in his shoulder holster.*

MAITLAND: Top quality meat?

> *Hunter moves to desk and picks*
> *up a file marked "CALLAN".*

HUNTER: He'll want the best...

CALLAN MAIN TITLE SEQUENCE

INT. CALLAN'S FLAT. DAY

Close up of Callan's gun on table. A box of ammunition is placed next to it. Pan out to see Callan and Lonely.

CALLAN:	You look worried.
LONELY:	That's the second box this month, Mr Callan.
CALLAN:	So what?
LONELY:	My wholesaler's beginning to ask questions.
CALLAN:	Change him.
LONELY:	He's reliable, Mr Callan.
CALLAN:	And nosey too. We can't have that in our business.
LONELY:	I don't even know what our business is.
CALLAN:	Just as well. You'd only worry - and you know what that does to your halitosis.
LONELY:	What do you do with all them bullets?

Callan picks up the gun and fondles it.

CALLAN:	I practice, Lonely.
LONELY:	But what for, Mr Callan?
CALLAN:	In our business, sometimes people try to kill you. If you practice, they don't.

Callan points the gun at Lonely.

INT. SECTION HQ. DAY.

Bauer enters Hunter's office where Hunter and Maitland wait. Bauer looks over the bank of closed circuit monitors, then around the office.

BAUER:	Charming, charming. And so very functional.

He nods towards Maitland.

	He also is functional?
HUNTER:	Oh yes. I don't like risks, Bauer.

BAUER:	I also.
HUNTER:	Sit there.

Bauer sits, looks at Maitland.

BAUER:	You can hardly miss me from there, young man.
MAITLAND:	Hardly.
BAUER:	It will not be necessary to prove it, Maitland. They would give me £50,000 if I killed your chief. I shan't do so. Why? Because alive he is worth so much more to me.
HUNTER:	Let's have it, Bauer.
BAUER:	As you know, I have a scheme to plant an agent in East Germany.
HUNTER:	It's approved.
BAUER:	And the price?
HUNTER:	£10,000. If and when you get him there.
BAUER:	That is where I need your help. I need a diversion.
HUNTER*:*	*Behind his desk we see Hunter's hand twitch over a gun in an open drawer.*
	Go on.
BAUER:	I should like to drop a hint in East Berlin that we are going to plant our agent – a very delicate hint, you understand. Then the Reds will feel very proud of themselves when they work out what is going to happen – it would never do to make things too easy for them.
HUNTER:	Get on with it, man.
BAUER:	When they expect a victim, it becomes our business to supply one. When they catch him, they will be content – and a little careless. Then we will slip in the real agent – and nobody will suspect him, because the spy the British were sending has already been caught.
HUNTER:	Standard procedure for the other side, but it won't do for us. You see the difficulty, Maitland?
MAITLAND:	Yes sir.
BAUER:	You must think me very stupid, but I don't.
HUNTER:	You're not stupid, Bauer, but you're greedy – and that's made you careless.
BAUER:	I do hope not.
HUNTER:	I'm sure you do. It could kill you.
BAUER:	One day it will, no doubt. But how have I been careless in this?
HUNTER:	The victim, Bauer, the victim. When the East Germans catch him they'll interrogate him. And they'll do it well.
BAUER:	They are thorough. Yes.
HUNTER:	They'll get information out of him – if he has any. And if he hasn't...

108

BAUER:	Yes?
HUNTER:	They'll never believe a man is a spy if he has no information to give.
BAUER:	Then we'll send them a spy who has some information. Not the newest, of course, and not the best. But enough to be convincing.

Close-up on Maitland's surprised but silent reaction.

HUNTER:	You want us to select one of our men and then betray him?
BAUER:	He would not, of course, be a successful, or important man.
HUNTER:	And that's where it won't do for us. There's the germ of an idea there – but I can't have that. Not betrayal.
BAUER:	An agent's entire life is betrayal.
HUNTER:	Not by his own side. Don't you agree, Maitland?
MAITLAND:	It would leak out, sir. Good scheme though very bad for morale.
HUNTER:	There we are then, Bauer. Good scheme though. Sorry to turn it down.
BAUER:	
(Beat)	There is one way.
HUNTER:	Oh yes? What do you suggest?
BAUER:	I felt sure you would come to it in time....We must send Callan.

Hunter and Maitland react.

INT. CALLAN'S FLAT. DAY

Callan is with a lay-out of model soldiers. A buzzer sounds and he goes to the door intercom.

CALLAN:	Yes?
EVA:	
(SOV)	You're not very polite, Callan.
CALLAN:	Eva...?

He buzzes her in and she enters the flat.

EVA:	I have missed you.
CALLAN:	Yeah...A long time...
EVA:	
(looking round)	
	I even missed this flat. I must have liked you very much.
CALLAN:	You acted like it...
EVA:	Or I would never have come to clean up this place for you. Forgive me – I know English people are

	sometimes upset by these questions – but are you very poor?
CALLAN:	No, not any more.
EVA:	But why do you live here?
CALLAN:	It suits me.
EVA:	You will never have chic...
CALLAN:	I leave that to you.
EVA:	You are very wise, Callan.
CALLAN:	And you are very beautiful.
EVA:	When you say that it is like saying "Today is Saturday".
CALLAN:	It is.
(They sit down)	How long are you here for?
EVA:	I leave tonight.
CALLAN:	Quick visit.
EVA:	I have been here a whole week...working.
CALLAN:	Ah!
EVA:	What does it mean – Ah!?
CALLAN:	It means you'll get yourself knocked off one of these days – if you don't watch it.
EVA:	But I always watch it, Callan.
CALLAN:	I hope so.
EVA:	Are you really beginning to worry about someone?
CALLAN:	Sometimes I think I'd like to.

Eva stands and moves to table.

EVA:	I will cook dinner, like in the old days.

*Eva takes a small box from her bag
and places it on the table.*

CALLAN:	Eva, why did you come?
EVA:	To bring you a little present. It's on the table.
CALLAN:	Thanks.

*He goes to table and opens the box, takes
out a model soldier and examines it.*

EVA:	
(SOV)	I saw it and I couldn't resist it. I think you'll love it.

Callan laughs. Eva turns to him and smiles.

INT. SECTION HQ. DAY

*Close up on drawer in Hunter's desk. A file
is placed in and the drawer closed. Pan back
to reveal Hunter, Maitland and Bauer.*

BAUER:	But surely Callan is the obvious one. You've

110

	finished with him and he's a potential danger to you.
HUNTER:	Is he?
BAUER:	With his knowledge and his temperament, he must be. Do as I say and you are rid of the danger.
HUNTER:	Those are my reasons for using Callan. I still haven't heard yours.
BAUER:	My reasons?
HUNTER:	You worked with him once.
BAUER:	I did.
HUNTER:	You tried to cheat him.
BAUER:	That is in my record. You know all about that?
HUNTER:	I do indeed. What happened when Callan found out?
BAUER:	He beat me. Very badly. I was in hospital for a month.
HUNTER:	And he could have been in Siberia for life if you'd succeeded.
BAUER:	I did not succeed that time.
HUNTER:	In our business, revenge is a very dangerous luxury. You really hate Callan, don't you, Bauer?

(Bauer scowls in anger and resentment.)

	...How long do we have to set him up?
BAUER:	Two days. I must have Callan in Berlin in two days.
MAITLAND:	
(Shocked)	Two days!
BAUER:	Forgive me. I thought this scheme would be immediately acceptable to you. I have already leaked the news that an agent is on his way.
HUNTER:	You're trying to push us, Bauer. We'll let you know tomorrow.
BAUER:	You are very good. Believe me, Callan is the only –
HUNTER:	Don't go on, Bauer. Tomorrow. At your hotel. Show him out, Maitland.
MAITLAND:	
(Standing up)	Yes, sir!

INT. CALLAN'S FLAT. EVENING

Callan and Eva relaxing. Model
soldiers laid out on table.

EVA:	So you liked my present?
CALLAN:	He's marvellous. Hungarian Hussar, isn't he?

111

EVA:	Yes. There is a photograph at home somewhere of my grandfather. He wore a uniform just like that – before the First World War. I tell everyone my grandfather was a Count with a castle in the Carpathians and a palace in Budapest. He was not. He kept a shop. But the Russians shot him just the same.
CALLAN:	And your father?
EVA:	No. He was shot by the Germans.
CALLAN:	And so will you be if...
EVA:	Espionage is my business. It pays me well, but it has its risks, like any other. I had to see you before I go. Women are possessive about old flames.

Close up on Callan who remains silent,
looking down at his hands.

INT. SECTION HQ SHOOTING RANGE. EVENING

Hunter watches as Maitland shoots at targets.

MAITLAND:	Any news from the man tailing Callan, sir?
HUNTER:	No, Maitland, he's acting like a law-abiding citizen. Nothing we can use... At the moment he's entertaining a lady.
MAITLAND:	We can hardly just ask him, sir, can we?
HUNTER:	No, Maitland, we can hardly just ask him, can we?
MAITLAND:	But anything we do he's bound to suspect, isn't he?
HUNTER:	Betrayal is never easy, Maitland.

A phone on the wall rings. Hunter answers it.

HUNTER: *(He listens then hangs up)*	Charlie here.
	That lady Callan's entertaining, Maitland...
MAITLAND:	Yes, sir?
HUNTER:	It's a woman called Eva Faber. Hungarian father, English mother. Callan used to be quite fond of her...
MAITLAND:	Oh really, sir?

Maitland aims at a target.

| HUNTER: | You know, betrayal isn't so difficult after all. It's as simple as shooting. |
| *(Maitland fires)* | All you need is a steady hand. |

112

INT. BATHROOM OF CALLAN'S FLAT. NIGHT

Eva is refreshing her make-up in the mirror.

CALLAN: Oi. Something I want to ask you.
EVA: Yes?
CALLAN: I don't want to be nosey or anything...
EVA: Liar!
CALLAN: But this job you did – who was the opposition?
EVA: I can't tell you.
CALLAN: Was it Hunter?
EVA: If you don't know he can't hurt you.

*She concentrates on her reflection in the
mirror. Callan leaves the bathroom.*

INT. KITCHEN OF CALLAN'S FLAT. NIGHT

Callan enters and talks quietly to himself.

CALLAN: Hunter. That'll be the third time she's done him. Stupid. Our Colonel's not the sort to kiss and make-up. Better get Lonely to keep an eye on her till her plane leaves.

INT. SECTION HQ. NIGHT

*Maitland is on the telephone. It becomes
clear he is calling Bauer.*

BAUER:
(SOV) Bauer.
MAITLAND: Bauer? Maitland here. The Colonel asked me to give you a message.
BAUER:
(SOV) Yes?
MAITLAND: The chap we discussed will be going to West Berlin after all. Tonight or tomorrow.
BAUER:
(SOV) That is very good news.
MAITLAND: You will be taking the bait back with you. We'll tell you where to pick her up. You understand?
BAUER:
(SOV) Of course. Thank the Colonel for me.
MAITLAND: Will do. Take care of yourself, old man.

INT. CALLAN'S FLAT. NIGHT.

Callan answers knock on the flat door, sees who is there and tries to close the door but the handle of an umbrella appears, preventing closure and Callan relents.

CALLAN: Sorry mate, I've got too much insurance already.

Hunter enters.

HUNTER: Mind if I come in?

Hunter approaches the table where Callan's model soldiers are laid out in battle formation.

Casualties?

CALLAN: Yeah. Sometimes I get carried away.

HUNTER: *(Sniffing loudly)* How long have you been using perfume?

CALLAN: *(Shrugs)* Since I left the firm I've changed in lots of ways...

Hunter ignores him and concentrates on the model soldiers on the table, picking up the one Eva has given Callan.

HUNTER: Oh, it's a new one is it? Austrian Imperial Cavalry. About 1860, if I remember.

CALLAN: You know I keep forgetting how old you are. You carry it so well.

HUNTER: *(Holding up model)* This was a Hungarian regiment. You like Hungarians, Callan?

CALLAN: They the ones who invented goulash?

HUNTER: One came to see you tonight. Eva Faber. She left here at eleven.

CALLAN: How dare you! What are you implying?

HUNTER: Miss Faber was doing a little job for the West Germans. Nothing important, but she did it very well. We got on to her too late.

CALLAN: Yeah. She can cook too.

HUNTER: You and she are friends, I understand...

CALLAN: I don't work with her, Hunter.

HUNTER: It wouldn't matter if you did, old son. Not now. But do try not to pick your lady friends from among the opposition in future. It upsets me.

Hunter goes out. Callan closes the door and leans against it.

CALLAN: *(To himself)* He's on to you, Eva girl. You haven't got a chance. Hope you're doing your job properly, Lonely.

INT. HUNTER'S OFFICE. NIGHT.

MAITLAND:
(On phone)   Yes, yes.
(He hangs up)   It seems to have worked, sir. That chap who smells followed her all the way to the airport. He saw everything.

HUNTER: Good.

INT. CALLAN'S FLAT. NIGHT. Intercut with: PHONE BOX. NIGHT.

CALLAN:
(On phone)   Yeah?

LONELY:
(In phone box)   Mr Callan. Your friend managed to get on that plane to West Berlin.

CALLAN: What do you mean "managed"?

LONELY: Very wobbly she was. Lucky she had two mates to help her.

CALLAN: What two mates? Where did she meet them?

LONELY: Brought her all the way from the hotel. Both had an arm round her.

CALLAN: Lonely, this is important. What did you think?

LONELY: Well, I thought they were a couple of heavies. She looked as if she'd been drugged. If she was my friend, Mr Callan, I wouldn't be happy.

        Close up of Callan grim-faced as he hangs up.

INT. BAUER'S FLAT. DAY Intercut with INT. HUNTER'S OFFICE. DAY.

        Phone rings in Bauer's flat and he picks up.

BAUER: 'Allo?

        Intercut with Hunter and Maitland at Section HQ. Maitland speaking into phone.

MAITLAND: Hello, Bauer? It's Maitland in London. Can you hear me?

BAUER: Perfectly.

MAITLAND: Oh good. Your old chum's on his way. Flight BEA 379. Should get in to West Berlin at 11.30 your time. He'll call on Miss Faber.

BAUER:	Thank you, Mr Maitland. Thank you very much indeed.
MAITLAND:	Not at all. Up to you now, Bauer. Take care of yourself, old boy.

As Maitland hangs up, camera goes to extreme close up on Hunter's impassive face.

END OF PART ONE

INT. EVA'S FLAT. DAY.

*Close up on a hypodermic being prepared.
Pan back to reveal Bauer who opens a
door to admit Franz. They position
themselves around the doorway. Camera
picks up Eva. When door buzzer
sounds, she answers.*

EVA: *Wer ist da?*
CALLAN:
(SOV)   It's me, love. Callan.
EVA: Come in.

*Callan enters and is immediately jumped
by Franz, who pins his arms whilst Bauer
jabs the hypodermic into Callan's neck. The
effect is immediate. Callan collapses. Eva
rushes over to kneel by Callan's body.
Bauer grabs her arm.*

BAUER: You are a fool. This man is wanted by East
German Intelligence. Do you want them after you
too?
EVA: No.

Bauer pulls her to her feet.

BAUER: I know all about you and the job you did in
London. Forget about this. You understand?
EVA: Yes.

*Bauer moves in on Eva and strikes
her twice across the face.*

BAUER: Discipline, Miss Faber. We must have discipline.

*Bauer and Franz pick up the
inert Callan and drag him out.*

INT. CORRIDOR. DAY.

*Callan's feet dragging as he is dragged down
a corridor to the door of Bauer's flat.*

INT. BAUER'S FLAT. DAY.

*Bauer and Franz drag Callan inside
and throw him on to a bed.
As Callan stirs, Bauer leans over
and slaps his face.*

BAUER:	*Das ist dummheit.*
CALLAN:	Bauer.
BAUER:	As you see.
CALLAN:	What's the gag?
BAUER:	No gags with you, Callan. Not any more.
CALLAN:	Where's Eva?
BAUER:	At home, minding her own business.
CALLAN:	I thought she was...
BAUER:	Going to East Berlin? No, Callan. You are.
CALLAN:	*What?*
BAUER:	You are a spy for the British and you will be caught. I am sorry I shall not be there when they interrogate you. Their methods are very thorough.
CALLAN:	Why send me?
BAUER:	To relax their suspicious minds. Once they have you, they will not look for the real agent. Clever, eh?

*Bauer leans in and forces Callan's arm
up his back, twisting savagely.*

BAUER:	You will answer.
CALLAN: *(Gasping)*	Yeah, it's clever.
BAUER: *(Releasing his hold)*	Good. I am going out now. Franz here will watch you. If you try to escape he has orders to hurt you where it will not show.

*Bauer leaves. Callan turns his head to look at
Franz who is sitting on guard. We hear Callan's
thoughts as he assesses the situation.*

CALLAN: *(SOV)*	Big. Too big for me. This one would eat me...

Callan sits up and mimes drinking.

CALLAN:	Water.... *Wasser, bitte.*

*Warily, Franz fetches a glass of
water. Callan reaches for it.*

CALLAN:	*Dankeschön.*

*Franz knocks the glass away just as
Callan is about to drink. As he returns
to his seat, Callan stares at him.*

CALLAN:	One of these days I'll see you again, mate. And I'll give you an English lesson.

INT. EVA'S FLAT.DAY.

Eva is holding the phone and we hear a distorted voice from the caller's end.

VOICE: *Polizei.*

Eva lowers the phone slowly without answering but before she hangs up we hear the distorted voice again.

VOICE: *Polizei.*

INT. BAUER'S FLAT. EVENING.

Close up of Callan's face. We hear his thoughts.

CALLAN:
(SOV)
If Bauer puts you over the Wall, you'll confess. They know just how to make you. Then it's fifteen years in the nick – and no remission. Hunter won't exchange you. You've got to get out.

Callan looks left then right and sees Franz still on guard.

CALLAN:
(SOV)
No. I can't take him.

Bauer enters to relieve Franz, who stands and leaves. Bauer sits.

BAUER: Are you hungry? A little sick perhaps? In five hours you won't have to worry about your stomach, the Reds will have you. Or maybe you are scared? You will answer.

CALLAN: Yeah. I'm scared.

BAUER: So you should be. Not of me – I do not want you marked. It would make the East Germans suspicious. You must go to them unblemished.

CALLAN: Like a bride.

BAUER:
(Smiling thinly)
I forgot how amusing you can be. It will not help you with them...Nothing will help you with them.

CALLAN: Yeah. I know.

BAUER: I waited five years for this, Callan. Ever since you gave me that beating.

CALLAN: I should have killed you.

BAUER: No doubt the beating was more satisfying.

CALLAN: Yeah...You yelled like a woman.

BAUER: This time you will do the yelling.

Close up on Callan thinking.

119

CALLAN:	
(SOV)	You've got to get him to come to you, mate. It's no good waiting for Eva. She won't help you...Nobody will...You've got to work it so he hits you first.
CALLAN:	
(Live)	You doing this job for Hunter? How much is he paying you?
BAUER:	£20,000.
CALLAN:	Come of it, mate – more like ten.
BAUER:	But anyway, you cannot afford to buy me off.
CALLAN:	I know.
BAUER:	Would you like to beg?
CALLAN:	No.
BAUER:	You will suffer a great deal. You will have to tell the truth, and they will not believe you.
CALLAN:	I'll remember the way you yelled, Bauer. It won't be so bad then. Just like a woman. Begging. Pleading.
BAUER:	Be quiet.
CALLAN:	I never saw anything like it. Tears in your eyes. "Don't hit me," you said. "I swear I didn't mean it," you said.
BAUER:	
(Angry)	Be quiet!
CALLAN:	No, not even a woman. A naughty little girl caught stealing jam...

> *Bauer rushes in close and holding his gun by the barrel, uses it as a club, smashing it into Callan's ribs. Callan grabs him and they fight. Callan manages to land a crucial karate blow and Bauer falls, knocked out. Callan staggers back holding his ribs, clearly in pain.*

CALLAN:	But by God, you know how to hurt.

> *Callan picks up Bauer's gun and leaves.*

INT. DOCTOR'S SURGERY. NIGHT.

> *Callan is trying the windows of what is clearly a doctor's surgery. The second one he tries opens and he climbs in. He walks carefully into the middle of the darkened room, avoiding screens and a trolley. He hears a female voice speaking German.*

DR SCHULTZ: *(SOV)*	*Wer ist da?*
	A door opens and Dr Schultz enters, turning on the lights. She goes to the open window and closes it, then turns and looks around the room, concentrating on the curtain screens.
DR SCHULTZ:	*Wer sind sie?*
	Callan appears through the screens.
CALLAN:	Do you speak English?
DR SCHULTZ:	I spoke English before you were born. I am English...or I was.
	Callan moves to check the door.
CALLAN:	You alone?
DR SCHULTZ:	Yes.
CALLAN:	Damn! When's the doctor coming back?
DR SCHULTZ:	The doctor...?
CALLAN:	Heinrich Schultz, love. The one with his name on the big brass plate outside.
DR SCHULTZ:	He's never coming back.
CALLAN: *(Gentle)*	You're an old lady and all that, but don't lie to me.
DR SCHULTZ:	I hardly ever lie nowadays. I am too tired. My husband was shot by the Russians in 1945.
CALLAN:	Oh my God.
DR SCHULTZ:	Why did you want to see him?
CALLAN:	I saw his name on the door. I need a doctor...
DR SCHULTZ:	Will any doctor do?
CALLAN:	Yeah...It's not that complicated. Just messy.
DR SCHULTZ:	I'm a doctor.
CALLAN:	You – a doctor?
DR SCHULTZ:	You're not very flattering.
CALLAN:	Excuse me. I've been mixing with the wrong sort of people lately.
DR SCHULTZ:	I think you had better sit down and let me look at you.
	She motions Callan to sit on a couch. As he does, he takes Bauer's gun from his waistband.
CALLAN:	Why aren't you yelling for the police?
DR SCHULTZ:	I only do that after I've examined the patient – if at all. Now let's see what's wrong.
CALLAN:	I don't want to hurt you, Doctor, so don't try anything.
DR SCHULTZ:	I can't treat you if you hurt me, can I? Now come along and don't be silly.
	Callan looks at her, then takes the gun and puts it down on the couch.

CALLAN:	There.
	He opens his shirt. Dr Schultz examines him.
DR SCHULTZ:	You have two broken ribs.
CALLAN:	That's what I thought. Can you fix it?
DR SCHULTZ:	I can tape them up for you.
CALLAN:	Just fix it so I can move around.
DR SCHULTZ:	You should be in hospital – in bed.
CALLAN:	I should be in Bermuda with a blonde on each arm. But I'm not.
DR SCHULTZ:	
(Resigned)	I can tape your ribs so that you can get around.
CALLAN:	Do it then.
DR SCHULTZ:	But I have to know something first.
CALLAN:	Oh? What?
DR SCHULTZ:	How did it happen?
	Callan reaches out and picks up the gun.
CALLAN:	I got hit with this.
DR SCHULTZ:	I see. And the man who hit you?
CALLAN:	I clobbered him. Look, Doctor, please…
DR SCHULTZ:	You hit him *after* he did that to you?
CALLAN:	Yeah. I set it up like that; made it happen. It was the only way I could get him to come to me.
DR SCHULTZ:	You are a remarkable young man.
CALLAN:	I'll be a dead young man if you don't fix my ribs.
DR SCHULTZ:	
(Looking at gun)	I have to report this to the police.
CALLAN:	No.
DR SCHULTZ:	I have no choice.
CALLAN:	Oh yes you have.
DR SCHULTZ:	I don't know why, but I'm almost certain you won't shoot me.
CALLAN:	Almost might not be good enough.
DR SCHULTZ:	Do you know, I think I'll risk that.
CALLAN:	All right, but I'll have to lock you up.
DR SCHULTZ:	But you can't go around like that. A broken rib can cause a serious injury.
CALLAN:	You're giving me no choice.
DR SCHULTZ:	It's very unfair to blackmail me just because I have a conscience.
CALLAN:	If I fight fair, I always lose. Please?
	Dr Schultz begins to treat Callan's ribs.
DR SCHULTZ:	Very well. No police. Not yet.

INT. BAUER'S FLAT. NIGHT.

> *Bauer and Maitland pace the room. They look at the bed where Callan had been.*

MAITLAND: He got away, didn't he? I told you twice to take care of yourself, Bauer. The deal's off.
> *Maitland storms out into the corridor with Bauer following.*

BAUER: Wait! Wait!

INT. CORRIDOR. NIGHT.

BAUER: He can't have got far. I hurt him.
> *Maitland gives him a card.*

MAITLAND: I'm at this number. Find Callan and we'll talk and this time, for God's sake, do as I say. Take care of yourself, old chap. You look terrible.

INT. DOCTOR'S SURGERY. NIGHT

> *Dr Schultz is preparing to treat Callan. She is holding a hypodermic syringe.*

CALLAN: What now?

DR SCHULTZ: I'm going to give you an injection.

CALLAN:
(Standing quickly, wincing with pain) No you're not.

DR SCHULTZ: I'm old. My hands are more clumsy than they used to be. I'll hurt you.

CALLAN: I've just been hurt, love. By an expert.

DR SCHULTZ: Very well. Sit down.
> *Dr Schultz moves to a wall cabinet, takes out a bottle and fills a tumbler.*

DR SCHULTZ: Drink this.

CALLAN: What is it?

DR SCHULTZ: For Heaven's sake...Schnapps. Very good Schnapps.

CALLAN: Thanks.

(He drinks) You're right.

DR SCHULTZ: Finish it. Did you really mean it – someone is trying to kill you?

123

CALLAN:	Just about.
DR SCHULTZ:	Then why don't you let me call the police?
CALLAN:	For all I know the police could be helping him.
DR SCHULTZ:	You're a criminal?
CALLAN:	No.
DR SCHULTZ:	I'll treat the lacerations first...Berlin has been full of spies for the last twenty years. They are almost commonplace.
CALLAN:	Like rats in a sewer.
DR SCHULTZ:	I suppose they are necessary...My husband was a Social Democrat. The Nazis hated him. He resisted them, you see. If he'd not been an exceptionally fine doctor he would have gone to Belsen.
CALLAN:	And the Russians got him instead?
DR SCHULTZ:	Yes.
CALLAN:	What had he done?
DR SCHULTZ:	Tried to protect me. Twenty-two years ago I was still quite handsome.
CALLAN:	It must have been rough here, all right.
DR SCHULTZ:	I'd almost forgotten the British genius for understatement! Now drink up.

> *Callan finishes the Schnapps.*
> *Dr Schultz takes the tumbler.*

DR SCHULTZ:	You still you don't want an injection?
CALLAN:	No.
DR SCHULTZ:	Very well. This is the part that is going to hurt. Please try to sit as still as possible. And try not to shout. Someone might here you outside.
CALLAN:	I won't shout.
DR SCHULTZ:	Very well.

> *She begins to strap Callan's ribs. Callan winces*
> *and flinches in pain but remains silent.*

DR SCHULTZ:	You're being very brave.
CALLAN:	
(Gasps)	Thanks.
DR SCHULTZ:	I'm afraid this is the bad one.
CALLAN:	Just get it done, love.
DR SCHULTZ:	Good boy...It's almost over.

> *As she pulls the last bandage tight, Callan*
> *slumps forward as he faints. Dr Schultz*
> *catches his upper body and lays him back*
> *on the trolley. She looks at the gun lying*
> *on the trolley, then looks at the unconscious*
> *Callan. She picks up the gun.*

END OF PART TWO

INT. DR SCHULTZ'S BEDROOM. NIGHT.

> *Close up of old Schultz family photographs in*
> *frames on chest of drawers. Includes one of*
> *man in WWI German uniform. Pan back to*
> *reveal Callan lying on bed, Dr Schultz*
> *leaning over him. Callan begins to come round.*

DR SCHULTZ: How do you feel?

CALLAN: Terrible.

(He turns his head
and looks round) How did I get here?

DR SCHULTZ: I wheeled you in.

CALLAN: You called the coppers?

DR SCHULTZ: No. Not yet.

CALLAN: Why not?

DR SCHULTZ: I didn't think that would be fair.

> *She helps Callan sit up.*

CALLAN: You're a caution, love.

DR SCHULTZ: Am I? I don't think I know enough about you to call the police yet, Mr Callan.

CALLAN: Have you been through my pockets, Doctor?

DR SCHULTZ: It was on your air ticket. All women are inquisitive you know. Even woman doctors. I wanted to know more about you before I sent for the police.

CALLAN: Know what?

DR SCHULTZ: Why. All I've discovered so far is that you're being hunted and that you have a very high tolerance to pain...and that...

CALLAN: Go on.

DR SCHULTZ: That you're as wary as an animal. You...Excuse me, I was going to be rude.

CALLAN: Go on. Don't stop now.

DR SCHULTZ: A long time ago my husband and I used to go on trips to the Bavarian forests. We used to watch animals and photograph them. Foxes, badgers – hawks too sometimes. Heinrich was very good at it. He published a book...it was a new technique in those days. You are very like those animals. The way you watch and listen. Your body is always ready to fight for you, isn't it? Just like a fox's.

CALLAN: I hope so.

125

| DR SCHULTZ: | I'm glad my children didn't get like that. |
| CALLAN: | You've got a family? Here? |

She shakes her head sadly.

| DR SCHULTZ: | Two sons. One killed over Coventry, the other at Stalingrad. I'm all alone and at your mercy. |

Callan sits up and swings his legs over the edge of the bed.

CALLAN:	I'm as weak as a kitten...You didn't drug me? When I was out?
DR SCHULTZ:	No, it's shock. It'll pass off.
CALLAN:	It better. I've got to get out of here.
DR SCHULTZ:	Mr Callan, please. I must ask you this. Why is this man chasing you?
CALLAN:	He needs me. He needs me for a job he's doing.
DR SCHULTZ:	A crime?
CALLAN:	No, love. But it ought to be...give me five minutes and I'll get out of your life.
DR SCHULTZ:	Where will you go?
CALLAN:	Templehof Airport. They can't touch you when you fly BEA... Where's my gun?

She moves to a chest of drawers, picks up the gun and hands it to Callan who hefts it, feeling its weight.

DR SCHULTZ:	It's here.
CALLAN:	Ahh! Where are the bullets, Doctor?
DR SCHULTZ:	I am sorry. There can be no more killing here. Not any more. I dropped them down the drain.
CALLAN:	
(Resigned)	That's all right, love. I respect your feelings.
(Stern)	But why the hell didn't you shoot me first?

INT. EVA'S FLAT. NIGHT

Bauer and Franz are confronting Eva.

BAUER:	He didn't come back?
EVA:	No.
BAUER:	Or telephone?
EVA:	No.
BAUER:	
(Moving in on Eva)	You wouldn't lie to me? No, not now. You wouldn't dare to lie, would you? I shall leave Franz here to look after you. Just in case Callan should come here and be troublesome. Don't worry, Franz won't do anything – if you don't.

Close up on Franz grinning.

INT. DR SCHULTZ'S BEDROOM. NIGHT.

Callan is walking gently up and down the room, clutching his ribs, clearly in pain.

CALLAN: It's no good. It hurts like hell.

DR SCHULTZ:
(Pleading) An injection ...

CALLAN: No!

DR SCHULTZ: Just a pain-killer...

CALLAN: I can't trust you.

DR SCHULTZ: I didn't call the police, did I?

CALLAN: You got rid of the bullets.

DR SCHULTZ: I've seen too many men die!

CALLAN: We all have! There's no novelty in it. But I don't want to die myself – and I don't want you to die either.

DR SCHULTZ: It isn't all that important when you're alone.

CALLAN: It is to me.

DR SCHULTZ: We watched it all happen in this street. First the Jews, then the Socialists. The beatings, the arrests, disappearances. Then the bombs falling, and the Gestapo at the door because I was born English and I might be a spy... My husband spoke out against it all.

CALLAN: Did he?

DR SCHULTZ: I told you.

CALLAN: Yeah...you told me. Was it true?

DR SCHULTZ: That's very cruel.

CALLAN: I'm sorry. I've been too busy just surviving. I forgot there was something better. But the ones who try it always get clobbered.

DR SCHULTZ: But so do you, Mr Callan. When my husband was an officer in the First World War...

CALLAN: In the army was he?

She goes to photographs on display on chest of drawers, selects one and offers it to Callan.

DR SCHULTZ: Yes. He finished his medical studies when it was over. This is Heinrich.

CALLAN:
(As he takes the picture) He's carrying a pistol.

DR SCHULTZ: All officers did.

CALLAN: All officers kept them too, didn't they?

DR SCHULTZ: Yes.

CALLAN: Have you still got it, Dr Schultz? Please get it for me.

DR SCHULTZ: No.

CALLAN: I've got to have it.

127

DR SCHULTZ:	Why don't you just leave? You're stronger now. I won't tell anybody I've seen you.
CALLAN:	They're looking for me. I could go out now and walk straight into them. I've got to have a gun. You think I won't hurt you. But suppose you're wrong this time? I'm scared rotten. That makes a difference.
DR SCHULTZ:	Mr Callan, you're in no condition to hurt anybody, not even an old woman.
CALLAN:	Doctor, it's the only chance I've got. Please don't make me...
DR SCHULTZ:	You won't hurt me. And I can't let you kill. I can't.
CALLAN: *(Holding photograph)*	What about your husband? Didn't he ever kill?
DR SCHULTZ:	Yes, he killed a Russian defending me – and the rest of them shot him, here in this house. The Russian died and Heinrich died and it didn't help me. Killing never helps.
CALLAN: *(Quiet but firm)*	How did he kill him?
DR SCHULTZ:	It was horrible.
CALLAN:	Did he use his pistol?
DR SCHULTZ: *(Shaking her head slowly)*	There wasn't time to get it.
CALLAN:	He'd hidden it.
DR SCHULTZ: *(Nods)*	Yes.
CALLAN:	Then it's still here. I'd better start looking, then, hadn't I? Tell me when I'm getting warm.

> *Energised, Callan moves rapidly around the room searching. He pulls open drawers, opens cupboards, moves furniture with fierce concentration. He fails to notice Dr Schultz sink down into a chair, a look of sad resignation on her face.*

INT. BAUER'S FLAT. NIGHT.

> *Bauer is on the phone.*

BAUER:	*Frau Doktor Schultz. Eine Engländerin? Danke.*

> *The doorbell buzzes. Bauer hangs up and crosses to open door to admit Maitland.*

MAITLAND:	Do you live on the phone, Bauer? I've been trying

	to get you for half an hour. We're running out of time.
BAUER:	I'm doing my best. There are fifty-four doctors in West Berlin that he hasn't been to.
MAITLAND:	The Colonel thinks we'd better forget the whole thing.
BAUER:	There's still an hour...
MAITLAND:	That depends on who he's talked to.
BAUER:	Who can he talk to? Who will believe him?
MAITLAND:	That's for you to find out, if you want the money.
BAUER:	
(Thinking)	Mr Maitland...
MAITLAND:	Yes?
BAUER:	There is another way.
MAITLAND:	Is there?
BAUER:	We could deliver the girl instead.
Maitland smiles.	
	Have I said something amusing?
MAITLAND:	No, no, not at all. It's just that half an hour ago the Colonel said you'd probably make that suggestion.
BAUER:	Well?
MAITLAND:	It wouldn't work if Callan gets away. He'll tip off the East Germans. The girl's important to him.
BAUER:	Forgive me. I don't think the girl is the only thing that's important to him.
MAITLAND:	Then why did he come to Berlin?
BAUER:	To put Hunter in his place.
MAITLAND:	
(Acknowledging Bauer's point)	He did it very nicely, didn't he...? Look Bauer, find Callan. But if you've roughed him up too much, send the girl – but only if you find Callan in time.
BAUER:	If he's too rough to send East – do I send him back to you?
MAITLAND:	
(Dismissive)	No. He doesn't belong to us any more.

INT. DR SCHULTZ:'S BEDROOM. NIGHT.

> *Callan searching room. He stands in front of a wardrobe, opens it and searches than stands back and reaches up to the top.*

CALLAN:	Getting hotter am I? Pass me the chair, love.
DR SCHULTZ:	No.

*Callan drags a chair across the floor to the
wardrobe and stands on it. He reaches on to
the top of the wardrobe and finds a gun
wrapped in cloth. As he retrieves it he winces
in pain and clutches his ribs with his left hand.*

CALLAN:
(In pain)   Aghh!
DR SCHULTZ: Careful!
*Dr Schultz rushes to help him, puts an arm
around him and leads him to the bed. Callan sits.*

CALLAN: You're a funny one. What did you want to help
me for?
DR SCHULTZ: I'd sooner do that than tape you up again.
Callan looks at her in admiration.

CALLAN: Dr Schultz – you believe in doing good to people,
don't you?
DR SCHULTZ: I try to.
CALLAN: How did you manage to stay alive so long?
DR SCHULTZ: I never thought about it.
CALLAN: And I never thought about anything else.
*Callan unwraps the cloth around the gun on his
knees to reveal an old Luger. He takes out the
magazine and ejects two rounds of ammunition.*

CALLAN: Your husband looked after it, but you didn't, love.
It's beginning to rust. I'll have to clean it. Where
are the rest of the bullets?
DR SCHULTZ: That's all there are.
CALLAN: Doctor, please. Don't start again...
DR SCHULTZ: I give you my word. If things got too bad – we
only needed two.

CALLAN:
(Sympathetic)   I'm sorry, doctor. Honest.
DR SCHULTZ: We never used them.
CALLAN: Maybe I won't either.
DR SCHULTZ: No, I think you want to. Now I'm sorry.
*She turns away as Callan tries to load
Bauer's gun with the bullets from the Luger.*

CALLAN: Wrong size ammo. I'll have to clean the Luger.
*In the Surgery the phone rings.
Dr Schultz looks at Callan.*

DR SCHULTZ: Should I answer?
CALLAN:
(Firm)   No.
DR SCHULTZ: It could be an emergency.
CALLAN: If it is, they'll call another doctor.
Phone stops ringing.

130

CALLAN:	Look, the man who's looking for me knows I'm hurt. He'll ring all the doctors round here just in case.

The phone starts to ring again. Dr Schultz automatically moves to answer it.

CALLAN: *(Hard)*	I said no.
DR SCHULTZ:	Somebody may need me.
CALLAN:	Somebody does, love. Me. And the opposition know it.

Phone keeps on ringing.

INT. BAUER'S FLAT. NIGHT

Bauer on phone. Maitland pacing, checking his watch.

BAUER:	No reply. This is the last one. I got word about her from a friend. She's English.
MAITLAND:	Really?
BAUER:	Dr Schultz. An old woman. She doesn't practice any more.
MAITLAND:	Does she live on the ground floor?
BAUER:	How should I know?
MAITLAND:	It would do no harm to find out. From what you tell me Callan was in no fit state to go climbing.

Bauer picks up a gun and checks it.

BAUER:	You'll come with me?
MAITLAND: *(With mock horror)*	Good Heavens no. He's all yours, old boy.

INT. DR SCHULTZ'S BEDROOM. NIGHT.

Dr Schultz looking at photograph of her husband. She places it back among her other pictures. Callan is cleaning and checking the Luger.

DR SCHULTZ:	Tonight taught me a lot about myself and Heinrich. I – I don't say I enjoyed talking to you, but I needed to.
CALLAN: *(Getting to his feet)*	Me too. I mean that.

DR SCHULTZ:	I don't practice now. It was good to be able to do something useful again.
	Dr Schultz helps him put on his jacket, but looks away in distaste as Callan puts the Luger into the waistband of his trousers.
CALLAN:	Thanks. You're right, Doctor. You know that. You'll always be right. And I'll always be wrong. And I can't change.
	Callan opens door to Surgery.
CALLAN:	Well, then...
DR SCHULTZ:	Write to me when you get to London. Just so I know you're safe.
	Callan leans forward and kisses her.
CALLAN:	I will.
	Callan turns to go then freezes as the doorbell rings. Dr Schultz moves behind him and they look into the empty Surgery as the bell rings insistently.
DR SCHULTZ:	I needn't answer ...
CALLAN:	
(Hard)	You must. They'll have seen the light.
	Callan lets her pass him. She goes into the Surgery and stands behind the door as the bell rings again.

SCENE INTERCUT WITH BAUER: IN HALLWAY OUTSIDE SURGERY DOOR.

DR SCHULTZ:	*Ja, bitte?*
BAUER:	Dr Schultz? I must come in please.
DR SCHULTZ:	But I don't take patients now.
BAUER:	It's very urgent.
	She opens door and Bauer pushes his way in. Callan watches through the bedroom door slightly open. He carefully and quietly cocks the action of the Luger.
DR SCHULTZ:	You know I'm English, I see.
BAUER:	I know all about you, Doktor Schultz.
DR SCHULTZ:	How terrifying. But if you want a doctor, I suggest you –
BAUER:	I am perfectly well. I'm looking for a man. An Englishman. He had an accident. He hurt his

	ribs. He would have had to visit a doctor for treatment.
DR SCHULTZ:	He didn't come to me.
BAUER:	
(Suspicious)	No?
DR SCHULTZ:	I've been alone here.

> *Bauer stalks the Surgery, picks up the tumbler Callan drank schnapps from and sniffs it.*

BAUER:	All evening? Drinking schnapps? You are a schnapps drinker. Doktor Schultz?
DR SCHULTZ:	Sometimes. I...
BAUER:	
(Menacing)	Let me smell your breath, Doktor...
DR SCHULTZ:	Really, you have no right to...
BAUER:	
(Grabbing at her)	Oh, but I have. Let me show you my warrant.

> *Bauer pulls out his gun and holds it close to her face. Dr Schultz pulls away from him.*

BAUER:	Come here.
(Bauer grabs her again and shakes her violently, shouting into her face)	
	Where is he? The man whose ribs you bandaged. The man who drank the schnapps. Where is he?

INTERCUT WITH CALLAN'S FACE THROUGH CRACK IN BEDROOM DOOR.

BAUER:	I have very little time, Doktor. Where is he?
DR SCHULTZ:	He didn't come here.

> *Bauer slaps her twice across the face. She staggers back and drops to her knees.*

BAUER:	You're lying.

> *Close up on Callan's face through crack. Sound of his thoughts.*

CALLAN:	
(SOV)	What are you waiting for? Get in there, mate. Get in there.

> *Callan pulls open the door and bursts into the Surgery holding the Luger.*

CALLAN:	Doctor! Stay down!

133

Callan fires twice. Bauer staggers back against
the wall and slumps to the floor. Callan
stands impassive. Dr Schultz crawls
across the floor to the body.

DR SCHULTZ: He's dead.
CALLAN: Yeah.
DR SCHULTZ: The heart – and the head.
CALLAN: That way you're sure.
                 Callan helps her to her feet and leads
                 her to a couch where she sits down.

DR SCHULTZ: You shoot very well.
CALLAN: So did he.
DR SCHULTZ: You didn't give him a chance.
CALLAN: He was hurting you.
DR SCHULTZ: I wanted you to stop him, yes – but not to kill
                 him.
CALLAN: What did you expect me to do? Challenge him to
                 a duel?
DR SCHULTZ: Couldn't you have wounded him?
CALLAN: No love. They never taught me how to wound.
                 Only how to kill.
                 Dr Schultz stares sadly at Callan as he
                 crosses to Bauer's body and picks up Bauer's
                 gun. He keeps that gun but places the Luger on
                 the couch next to her. Dreamily she reaches
                 out and places her hand over it.

CALLAN: Can I use your phone?
                 Dr Schultz takes her hand quickly
                 off the Luger and waves Callan towards
                 the telephone. He picks it up and dials.

INTERCUT CALLAN IN DR SCHULTZ'S SURGERY with EVA in her FLAT – both on phone.

EVA: *Ja?*
CALLAN: Callan. You alone?
EVA:
(Looks around flat
to see Franz)   Not really.
CALLAN: Bauer's dead.
EVA: His friend is here. You'd better tell him.
CALLAN: Franz? Put him on.
                 In Eva's flat she hands the phone to Franz.

CALLAN:	Franz? Here's the English lesson I promised you. *Eine durch das Herz.* One through the heart. *Und eine durch den Kopf.* And one through the head. He'll never be deader.
	Behind Callan, Dr Schultz gasps in horror.
EVA: *(Back on phone, now alone)*	He's gone. You're very convincing
CALLAN:	The truth always is.
EVA:	Thank you, Callan.
CALLAN:	Why thank me? I was the one they were really after.
EVA:	Are you all right?
CALLAN:	I'll do.
EVA:	Where are you? I'll come to you.
CALLAN: *(Sharp)*	No!
EVA:	But I want to help you, my gallant hussar.
CALLAN:	You should have yelled out sooner, love. Then we'd all have been gallant.
	Callan hangs up suddenly.

INT. EVA'S FLAT. NIGHT.

Eva holding a disconnected phone.

EVA:	Callan! Callan!

She slowly replaces the receiver.

INT. DR SCHULTZ'S SURGERY. NIGHT.

CALLAN:	I've got to go.
DR SCHULTZ:	You talked about him as if he were a sheep – and you worked in a slaughter house.
CALLAN:	I do.
DR SCHULTZ:	I wanted to like you. But now...
	Callan takes a coat that has been hanging behind the door and holds it for Dr Schultz to put on.
CALLAN:	Yeah. It's as well we didn't get to know each other better. I'm taking you to the airport with me. You can call the coppers from there when I've gone and tell them what happened.

Dr Schultz stands up and slips into
the coat Callan is holding for her.

DR SCHULTZ: All of it?
CALLAN: Yes.

He guides her to the door, an arm round her.

DR SCHULTZ: Your name, too?
CALLAN: Callan? There's no such person, love. He doesn't
                  exist.

As they go through the Surgery door,
END CREDITS *roll.*

Blackmailers Should Be Discouraged

by

James Mitchell

Editor's Introduction

As with *Goodness Burns Too Bright,* the 'lost' episode *Blackmailers Should Be Discouraged* from the second season of *Callan,* is reconstructed from a studio shooting script, which is packed with technical directions for camera angles and the positioning of microphones, but from which almost all dramatic directions have been removed.

Several pages have been replaced and others badly damaged, leaving minor gaps in the flow of scenes. For several scenes, there is little indication from the camera script as to what the actors are actually doing, which they would have decided in rehearsal. A filmed insert is listed as lasting almost three minutes of finished screen time, yet the only dramatic direction for Callan and the character Todd is "Fight Sequence".

I have attempted to reconstruct the script as I hope James Mitchell would have envisaged it, retaining all his dialogue, although I have never seen this episode. Any mistakes and misinterpretations are, consequently, entirely mine.

Blackmailers Should Be Discouraged

A *Callan* episode

Recorded at ABC Television's Teddington Lock Studios on 18th &19th June 1968.

Broadcast as Episode 8 of Season 2 of *Callan* on 26th February 1969. No known copy of this recording exists.

CAST:

Callan	....	EDWARD WOODWARD
Hunter	....	DEREK BOND
Lonely	....	RUSSELL HUNTER
Sir Gerald Naylor	....	NICHOLAS SELBY
Lady Naylor [Ruth]	....	KARIN MacCARTHY
Ritchie	....	JOHN FRANKLYN ROBBINS
High Commissioner	....	JOHN ARNOTT
Bishop	....	JOHN WOODNUTT
Benson	....	DENIS THORNE
Todd	....	BARRY ANDREWS
Toastmaster	....	BERNARD WHITEHORN

Associate Producer .... John Kershaw

Executive Producer .... Reginald Collin

Directed by .... James Goddard

Note: INT. means the scene is an Interior setting (as opposed to **EXT.** or exterior) and **SOV.** means *Sound of Voice* only when an actor is off-screen or to illustrate thought rather than direct speech; similarly, **V/O** is Voice Over. **FX** refers to Sound Effects such as traffic noise, chatter at a party, sound of machinery etc.

OPENING TITLES

INT. HUNTER'S OFFICE. EVENING.

> *Close up on a CCTV monitor [FX: distant traffic].*
> *Monitor comes to life and we see a formal dinner/banquet*
> *scene. [FX: laughter, applause, chatter]. We see a*
> *liveried TOASTMASTER call for order, banging a gavel.*

TOASTMASTER:
(on CCTV screen)

Your Eminence, Your Excellencies, Your Grace, my lords, ladies and gentlemen... Pray silence for your chairman, Sir Gerald Naylor....

> *On monitor screen, a dinner-jacketed*
> *speaker (NAYLOR) stands at microphone.*
> *[FX; applause].*

NAYLOR:
(on screen)

Your Eminence, your...

> *Camera pulls back to reveal bank of four*
> *CCTV monitors all showing live pictures*
> *form the dinner/banquet.*

HUNTER:
(SOV)
NAYLOR:
(on screen)

Oh my God, not again.

...Excellencies, your Grace, my Lords, Ladies and Gentlemen. Once I have said all that I feel as though my speech is almost over.

(FX: laughter)

As you know, this is my swan song. My wife and I will shortly be leaving for Canada where I shall be in charge of the Nuclear Research Division of the Three Power atomic project.

(FX: applause)

At such a time it is, I think, always as well...

> *Camera pulls back to reveal, from the back,*
> *the heads and shoulders of HUNTER and*
> *CALLAN looking at monitors.*

HUNTER:
CALLAN:

You got enough of him?
Yes. As much as I need.

HUNTER:	Good.
	(He leans over and switches off the sound on the monitors)
	Scientists make even worse after-dinner speeches than judges.
CALLAN:	Naylor hasn't been a scientist for twenty years. He's an administrator.
HUNTER:	He talks their language anyway. And they did make him chairman of their society.
CALLAN:	You're letting him go to Canada, then?
HUNTER:	That rather depends on you. The CIA were on to me again today. Security-wise, are we one hundred per cent sure?
CALLAN:	In other words, they've got nothing to go on?
HUNTER:	Just a hunch. A feeling.
CALLAN:	I can't check up on a feeling.
HUNTER:	There is something more.
	HUNTER reaches into his jacket inside pocket and produces a sheet of paper which he hands to CALLAN, who unfolds it and reads.
CALLAN:	"Sir Gerald Naylor is a Communist traitor. His sexual activities are disgusting". He gets an awful lot out of twelve words, this bloke. I bet he sends a marvellous telegram.
HUNTER:	The message is typed, as you see. No signature, no address.
CALLAN:	Who was it sent to?
HUNTER:	The High Commissioner. He passed it on to us with the greatest reluctance. He despises anonymous letters.
CALLAN:	Where's the envelope?
HUNTER:	Being analysed. It was typed too. I doubt it will tell us anything.
CALLAN: *(Waves sheet of paper)*	Anything in all this?
HUNTER:	If he's a Communist, he's hidden it damn well. Oh, I agree. A lot of them do.
CALLAN:	What about the disgusting sexual activities?
HUNTER:	It seems he keeps them hidden too. His wife might know, of course.
CALLAN:	What am I supposed to do, sir? Go up and ask her?
HUNTER:	Do what you like, but find out.
	(He indicates the silent banquet scene on the monitors)

CALLAN: Do you think he's through yet?
HUNTER: I doubt it.
        So do I. All the same, we'd better get along to the reception. Are you going to tell him who you are?
CALLAN: I might, if I think it would frighten him. You're not giving me much time.
HUNTER: He's supposed to fly to Canada on Thursday.
CALLAN: I'd better frighten him then.
        (They both stand up and for the first time we realise that they are both wearing formal dinner jackets.)

HUNTER: Good Lord. You look quite elegant.
CALLAN: *(Tugging his jacket straight)* I may look it, but I'm not going to sound it.
HUNTER: Then keep your mouth shut.
        (HUNTER looks at CALLAN's jacket, then down at his own. On the breast pocket he has a row of medals. CALLAN has only one.)

        The invitation said specifically "Orders and decorations". Where are the "orders and decorations"?
CALLAN: It's taken me all this time to get into this monkey suit. And this is the only gong I've got.
HUNTER: It's too blatant for a diplomatic reception.
(HUNTER points to his medals)

        Now pick one I can spare.
        (CALLAN nods and HUNTER removes a medal and pins it on CALLAN.)

        There. That's the ticket.

INT. RECEPTION ROOM. NIGHT.

        (HIGH COMMISSIONER, HUNTER and CALLAN in middle of a formal reception with guests and waiters carrying trays of drinks. FX: chatter, laughter, background music.)

HIGH COMMISSIONER: Naylor should be here any time. How do I introduce you to him?
HUNTER: Not to me, your excellency. Just Callan here. Say he's with the Foreign Office. He quite often is, in a shady sort of way.
HIGH COMMISSIONER: I see.

HUNTER: He hates all this. They do, you know, all the decent chaps. And yet they use us.

CALLAN: Supposing Naylor isn't clean. What happens to him?

HUNTER: That depends on what he's done. If it's just routine I expect we'll retire him. Overwork. Strain on the heart. The usual.
(HUNTER looks to his left, surprised)

Good Lord!
(HUNTER sees LADY NAYLOR enter the reception followed by NAYLOR)

That is his wife?

CALLAN: You've seen her on the box.

HUNTER: But she looked quite ordinary, She's lovely. And so young.

CALLAN: We all want them like that. But most of us can't afford them.
(The HIGH COMMISSIONER escorts SIR GERALD and LADY NAYLOR across the room to introduce them to CALLAN. A waiter with a tray of drinks serves them.)

HIGH COMMISSIONER: Sir Gerald, may I present Mr Callan of your Foreign Office?

(To CALLAN) Sir Gerald Naylor.

CALLAN and NAYLOR:
(Together)
NAYLOR: How do you do?

(Easing his wife forward) My wife, Lady Naylor.

CALLAN and RUTH:
(Together, shaking hands) How do you do?

NAYLOR: Are the F.O. taking an interest in our activities, Mr Callan?

HIGH COMMISSIONER: Well, you know these Foreign Office fellas. You can't keep them away from a good party.
(HIGH COMMISSIONER spots a guest leaving and moves away to follow him)

Hey, wait a minute, Roy! I haven't even said hello yet...

NAYLOR: Which desk do you work at, Mr Callan?

CALLAN: I don't. I'm not attached.

NAYLOR: Excuse me.
(NAYLOR spots another guest, signals to him and abruptly walks away from

144

CALLAN. RUTH [Lady Naylor] steps
in to talk to CALLAN)

RUTH: Gerald isn't usually rude. Do forgive him, You see, the man he's talking to is Skindle.

CALLAN:
(Unimpressed) Really?

RUTH: I bet you haven't the slightest idea who Skindle is. He's a Fellow of Trinity and an FRS. One of the world's experts on heavy water.

CALLAN: Ah...

RUTH: Atoms and things.

CALLAN: Are you a scientist, Lady Naylor?

RUTH: No. I was my husband's secretary, Mr Callan. I think I've met every eminent physicist who ever came to this country, but I still can't understand a word they say.

CALLAN: Are you sorry to be leaving England?

RUTH: Oh no, my husband's job is very important, you know. And nowadays one can buy such lovely things in Canada.
(She spots NAYLOR waving at
her across the room)

Oh dear, my husband's waving me over. Goodbye, Mr Callan. So nice to have met you.

CALLAN:
(Gracious) It's been tremendous fun.
(RUTH walks off. HUNTER rejoins CALLAN
and watches her go to her husband)

HUNTER: Very, very lovely. I'm sure she means trouble.

CALLAN: Have you checked her out?

HUNTER: Whiter than white. Why do you ask?

CALLAN: She said herself she's met every eminent physicist there is. She's bored and she's ambitious.

HUNTER: All this in five minutes chat?

CALLAN: She wasn't making any effort to hide it.

HUNTER: I wonder if writing anonymous letters is a cure for boredom?

CALLAN: No. Not her. She values her husband's career too much.

HUNTER: All the same, you'd better run another check on her. No doubt you'll find it amusing.

CALLAN:	O.K. I'd better lean on Naylor tonight. He looks worried. It could be useful.
HUNTER:	
(Nodding towards an exit)	The little room along the corridor to the left. I'll see he's sent to you.

> *(CALLAN turns and weaves through the crowded room, glass in hand, towards the exit. On the way he lifts a bottle of champagne from a waiter's tray so smoothly the waiter does not notice. HUNTER checks the position of NAYLOR and RUTH, still talking to guests, then locates the HIGH COMMISSIONER and approaches him.)*

HUNTER:	Your Excellency, I hate to bother you again...

> *(HUNTER leans in close to the HIGH COMMISSIONER and whispers something in his ear)*

HIGH COMMISSIONER:	Look, Hunter, do you have to? Gerry Naylor is a friend of mine. I like the guy...
HUNTER:	Sir, I'm afraid I must. Callan wants a word with him. Alone.
HIGH COMMISSIONER:	What – now? At my reception? Get him down to your office tomorrow...
HUNTER:	There isn't time. Not if we have to check on that letter, sir.
HIGH COMMISSIONER: *(sighing)*	O.K. What do I have to do?

INT. STUDY. NIGHT.

> *(CALLAN enters and puts the champagne bottle down on a coffee table. Almost immediately, he turns to the doorway as NAYLOR enters)*

NAYLOR:	The High Commissioner said you wanted to see me.
CALLAN:	I do.
NAYLOR:	I must warn you I don't accept the Foreign Office's jurisdiction over our project.
CALLAN:	Whose do you accept, Sir Gerald?
NAYLOR:	What possible business is it of yours?
CALLAN:	Before we go any further, I think you'd better take a look at this.

(CALLAN produces an official Security Pass and shows it to NAYLOR)

NAYLOR: This gives you the authority to spy on me?

CALLAN: We like to call it security.

(NAYLOR pulls up a chair to the coffee table and fills his glass from the champagne bottle.)

NAYLOR: What am I supposed to have done?

CALLAN: *(Quizical)* That's your third glass since you met me. According to your file you don't usually drink like that.

NAYLOR: *(Angry)* What the hell am I supposed to have done?

CALLAN: Nothing. We're more concerned about what you *might* do.

(NAYLOR sinks down into the chair)

NAYLOR: Yes, do sit down. You do realise what this job means to me? It's as far as anyone with my qualifications can go.

CALLAN: It pays well too.

NAYLOR: That isn't what I meant.

CALLAN: It's what your wife means.

NAYLOR: My wife likes expensive things, and she's young and I'm not.

CALLAN: I hear you're a Red.

NAYLOR: *(Angry)* It's a damn lie.

CALLAN: I also hear you can be blackmailed.

NAYLOR: Blackmailed? For what?

CALLAN: Your sex life?

NAYLOR: *(Exasperated)* This is ridiculous. Listen to me, I was a scientist. I am now an administrator. Last year I got married. And that's my whole adult life. To most people it would be damn boring, apart from my marriage. But it has been useful. It will go on being useful. That's why I'm going to Canada.

CALLAN: If I let you.

NAYLOR: *(Shocked)* What?

CALLAN: You could be a risk, sir. It's up to me to decide. If you are – you don't go.

NAYLOR: But these accusations...They're fantastic. I demand to know who made them.

(CALLAN remains impassive)

Very well. I'll go to the High Commissioner.

CALLAN:	He calls you Gerry. He's a friend of yours, but he can't help you.
NAYLOR:	We'll see.
CALLAN:	We'll see.

INT. RECEPTION AREA. NIGHT.

(FX: chatter, background laughter, music. NAYLOR comes in fast, pushing violently through the party-goers, looking for the HIGH COMMISSIONER)

INT. STUDY. NIGHT.

(Shot of mirror hanging on wall. CALLAN comes in to frame and examines his face in the mirror)

CALLAN:
(To his reflection)

Oh mate. You've come a long way since the Scrubs.

INT. RECEPTION AREA. NIGHT.

(FX: chatter, laughter, music. NAYLOR has found the HIGH COMMISSIONER and is berating him)

NAYLOR:	But what that spy said...He accused me of ...
HIGH COMMISSIONER:	Gerald, calm down will you.
NAYLOR:	He called me a Red...
HIGH COMMISSIONER:	Take it easy. The whole place is looking at you.
NAYLOR:	I'm sorry, but he made the most fantastic accusations.
HIGH COMMISSIONER:	I know it.
NAYLOR:	Did he tell you what they were?
HIGH COMMISSIONER:	I know that too.
NAYLOR:	And you let him?
HIGH COMMISSIONER:	What choice have I got?

> *(NAYLOR, fuming, storms out. As he leaves RUTH rushes after him, calling out, but the HIGH COMMISSIONER calls her back.)*

RUTH: Gerald!
HIGH COMMISSIONER: Ruth...

INT. STUDY. NIGHT.

> *(CALLAN and NAYLOR confronting each other. CALLAN remains impassive.)*

NAYLOR: I don't believe it. I simply don't believe it.
CALLAN: Why not? It's happening.
NAYLOR: But it's got nothing to do with me.
CALLAN: You'd say that anyway.
NAYLOR: Alright. What do I have to do to prove I'm innocent?
CALLAN: Show me. Show me your life, Naylor. Show me how boring and useful it is.
NAYLOR: My records, d'you mean?
CALLAN: Records, snapshots, diaries...the lot.
NAYLOR: Tomorrow.
CALLAN: No, now. You and your wife would like to be on that plane.

INT. HUNTER'S OFFICE. DAY. (Early morning)

> *(CALLAN, dishevelled, is asleep in Hunter's chair. HUNTER puts a hand out on to Callan's shoulder and at the faintest touch, Callan draws his gun from his shoulder holster with lightning speed but then sees who it is. HUNTER pats him gently on the shoulder,)*

HUNTER: Comfortable?
> *(CALLAN rises and stretches and rubs his unshaven chin as he vacates Hunter's chair.)*

CALLAN: Well, it's the only decent chair in the place. What time is it?
HUNTER: Eight o'clock. How did you get on?
CALLAN: I didn't, I didn't. He's got a five-roomed flat in Belgravia, and a three-and-a-half

	litre sports – last year's model. The flat's seven hundred a year. The wife's got a mink, a diamond necklace and a lot of French perfume.
HUNTER: *(Suspicious)*	
CALLAN:	Very expensive...
	Yeah...Except that he had an aunt die two years ago and left him twenty thousand quid. It's all there – and that's all there is. Oh, and he's got three friends he plays bridge with once a fortnight.

> *(HUNTER looks quizzical but CALLAN shakes his head)*

	The nearest Naylor got to Communism was the Liberal Club.
HUNTER:	You're going to clear him?
CALLAN:	No. Not yet. He's playing it right. Half the time he's indignant, the rest he's baffled. But underneath he's worried out of his mind. You get any joy out of that envelope?
HUNTER:	Cheap stuff. So was the paper. Buy it anywhere.
CALLAN:	Postmark?
HUNTER:	None. It was delivered by hand. Marked 'For the Attention of the High Commissioner. Personal. Most urgent'. Look, Callan, it could be just spite, some enemy of his.
CALLAN:	I tell you, he's a jolly decent chap. He hasn't got any enemies.
(Beat)	And nobody's that clean.

INT. LONELY'S FLAT. DAY

> *(FX: distant traffic and children playing outside. Camera opens on LONELY in bed. At first only his foot, sticking out from under the bed clothes is visible.)*

CALLAN: *(SOV)*	Lonely! Lonely!
LONELY: *(Head emerges from covers)*	That you, Mr Callan?
CALLAN: *(SOV)*	No. It's Snow White. I've brought the seven dwarfs round for coffee. Open up, will you?

150

(LONELY sits up, then rolls out bed and stands. He is wearing torn and grubby underwear. He opens the door to admit CALLAN who is still wearing his dinner suit)

CALLAN:
(Looking around flat)   I thought you had a bit of grumble in here.
LONELY: I was asleep, Mr Callan.
CALLAN: You were lucky, mate.
LONELY: Ain't you been to bed, then, Mr Callan?
CALLAN: I don't even know what it looks like any more.

LONELY: Fancy a cup of coffee?
CALLAN: I'll make it.

(He notes the 'girlie' pin-ups stuck on the walls)

Put some clothes on for God's sake, Lonely. You gorgeous beast you. Don't you know all you need's a rose in your teeth and you can join the lovelies on the wall.

(CALLAN busies himself with a kettle and makes coffee.. He picks up one cup and holds it up to eye-level before handing it to LONELY.)

Hello. Dresden that is. You been thieving again?
LONELY: I got to live, Mr Callan.
CALLAN: I've got a job for you tonight. Twenty-five quid.
LONELY: I've got another job on.
CALLAN:
(Reacting)   You're scared, Lonely. I can smell it. It's easy, if I say it's easy – it's easy.
LONELY: It's the twenty-five quid, Mr Callan. I need a bit more.
CALLAN:
(Sigh)   How much?
LONELY: Three hundred quid.
CALLAN: Don't be daft. What would you need three hundred quid for?
LONELY: I got a lot of commitments.
CALLAN: (Looks around the scruffy flat)   Yeah, I can see you have. Lonely, you're not trying to put the screws on me are you?
LONELY: No, Mr Callan. I wouldn't do that. Honest. You been very good to me.

151

CALLAN:	Remember that, Lonely.
LONELY:	Any other night this week I'd have been happy to oblige you.
CALLAN: *(Shaking head)*	Sorry. It's got to be tonight. I'll have to do it on my own.
LONELY:	Do you mind if I give you a bit of advice? Get some kip first. You'll never do no tickle if you're half asleep.
CALLAN: *(Nodding in agreement)*	Yeah, right. Good luck for tonight.
LONELY:	You too, Mr Callan.
CALLAN:	Yeah.

> *(CALLAN leaves the flat. As soon as he has gone, LONELY goes to the mantelpiece and grabs a china vase which contains a roll of money. He counts it anxiously and looks worried.)*

EXT. OUTSIDE LONELY'S FLAT. DAY.

> *(As CALLAN leaves the building, he passes another man – TODD – entering. They eye each other warily but do not speak.)*

INT. LONELY'S FLAT. DAY

> *(LONELY is still by the mantelpiece counting his money over and over again. FX: knock at door)*

LONELY:	Who is it?

> *(Before he can open the door, it is kicked open and TODD barges in pushing LONELY back into the room.)*

TODD: *(Grinning)*	Todd.

> *(TODD advances as LONELY retreats, snapping his fingers in LONELY's face until LONELY reaches for the vase with the money and hands it over.)*

TODD:	There's only two hundred here. I want another three.

LONELY:	You'll get the rest tomorrow – like you said.
TODD:	Will I, Lonely? Will I really?
LONELY:	Cross my heart and hope to die.
TODD:	Because if I don't, the law will get to know who turned over Mike Kennedy's flat and you'll go inside. And when you come out, Mike will break your skull.

(LONELY, hands shaking, picks up his cup of coffee and tries to drink. TODD sees the Dresden china cup, reaches out and takes it, then throws the contents in LONELY's face. LONELY squeals.)

TODD:	How foolish you are, Lonely. How very foolish. That's Dresden, isn't it? The Pont Street job.
LONELY:	I like it. It's pretty.
TODD:	It's also evidence.

(He throws the cup to the floor where it smashes.)

Sweep up the pieces, Lonely. Put them in the bin. Somebody else's bin.

LONELY: *(Briefly defiant)*	You rotten git. I've got a friend who'd... fix you.
TODD:	Now, Lonely. No language. Not at me. Or I might let Mike Kennedy know before I told the law. And Mike would put you in hospital...

(Close up on LONELY's face and expression of fear.)

END OF PART ONE

INT. NAYLOR'S LIVING ROOM. NIGHT

(CALLAN is prowling the darkened room, using a flashlight. He examines a desk, checking the drawers then kneeling down and running a gloved hand around the knee-well.)

CALLAN:
(Muttering quietly)

Nothing. Nothing, Nothing.
(Callan rises and sits in the desk chair. He places his flashlight on the desk and the beam illuminates a cigarette box.)

CALLAN:
(Curious)

According to his file he doesn't smoke. Nor does Lady Naylor...
(CALLAN empties out the cigarettes and shines the flashlight on to the inside of the lid where there are two capital letters inscribed.)

CALLAN:
(Reading)

"G" and "I"...
(He hefts the box, turns it and examines the dimensions.)

The base – it's too thick...
(CALLAN runs a finger round the base of the box. There is a click and a secret compartment slides open. It contains a photograph of a group of three young men clearly in Cambridge, in a punt on the river Cam. CALLAN removes it and props it up against the box. He stands and takes a miniature camera from his pocket and photographs the picture.)

CALLAN:
(Resigned)

No, mate, nobody is that clean. You poor bastard.

INT. HIGH COMMISSIONER'S STUDY. DAY

(HUNTER enters the study and sits down opposite the HGH COMMISSIONER'S desk. He holds a print of the photograph CALLAN took.)

HIGH COMMISSIONER: I want you to lay off Naylor.

HUNTER: You are sure he's innocent?

HIGH COMMISSIONER: Of course I'm sure.

HUNTER: In spite of the anonymous letter you passed on to us.

HIGH COMMISSIONER: I should never have done that.

HUNTER: *(Dismissive)* Huh!

HIGH COMMISSIONER: You don't agree with me?

HUNTER: We found something else.

(HUNTER hands over the photograph. The HIGH COMMISSIONER examines it.)

HIGH COMMISSIONER: So what? A bunch of kids at Cambridge. I want you to drop this, Hunter.

HUNTER: I'm sorry, sir.

HIGH COMMISSIONER: *(As HUNTER rises to leave)* Look, I'm telling you to drop it.

HUNTER: *(Standing)* I really am sorry. The trouble is I've been in touch with my Minister. He wants me to go on.

HIGH COMMISSIONER: Doing what for God's sake?

HUNTER: Investigating this photograph. We've found out who one of the other two is.

HIGH COMMISSIONER: *(Angry)* Who? The head of Russian Intelligence?

HUNTER: No, he's a clergyman. Somewhere in Somerset. Let's hope he has a good memory...

EXT. COUNTRY CHURCH. DAY
(Establishing shot)

INT. CHURCH PORCH. DAY.

(CALLAN is introducing himself to a clergyman - the Vicar, RITCHIE.)

RITCHIE: Mr Callan.

CALLAN: Mr Ritchie.

RITCHIE: Did you have a good trip down?

CALLAN: Yes, fine.

RITCHIE: This is most unusual, you know. I am somewhat at a loss to understand how I can be of service to the Foreign Office.

CALLAN: It's a long shot, Mr Ritchie. It may not amount to much.

RITCHIE: Oh I do hope it may, I do hope it may. This village is what the Parish Council terms 'unspoiled' in a vain hope to attract the more affluent kind of resident. A more accurate definition would be dull. Even boring perhaps. Any intrusion from the great world must augur a little excitement. I should offer you refreshments, I know, but unfortunately sherry is beyond my means and my coffee is execrable. I am, besides, a very lazy man and since my poor wife died, I use the word 'poor' quite literally. Neither of us had twopence. I'm talking too much...

CALLAN: No. Oh, no. I want you to treat this as confidential, Mr Ritchie.

RITCHIE: Of course. In any case, my dear chap, no one under fifty talks to a parson any more, except to say 'I do' or 'I will'.

(He indicates that CALLAN should follow him)

This way.

INT. VESTRY. DAY

(The church vestry is cluttered with piles of hymn books, collecting boxes etc. There is a desk which is littered with papers, sellotape, scissors and office equipment including a portable typewriter. CALLAN and RITCHIE enter.)

CALLAN:	You were at Cambridge, weren't you?
RITCHIE:	To be sure. Three delightful years.

(CALLAN produces the photograph he took and hands it to RITCHIE)

CALLAN:	Do you remember this photograph?
RITCHIE:	God bless my soul. Isn't that Gerald Naylor?
CALLAN:	Yes.
RITCHIE:	Not in any trouble, is he?
CALLAN:	Sir Gerald? Why should he be?
RITCHIE: *(Correcting himself)*	Sir Gerald – of course. I read of his KCVC in a Birthday Honours – let me see – three years ago? And didn't he marry subsequently? A very comely young lady?
CALLAN:	Lady Naylor is very pretty.
RITCHIE:	My dear chap, my very dear chap, mere prettiness would never do for Gerald.
CALLAN:	You didn't like him?
RITCHIE:	What makes you say that? I admired him enormously. It is good to find that he has at last found time for the...er...gentle sex.
CALLAN:	He didn't when you knew him?
RITCHIE:	He was so dedicated to his work – he took an excellent double first, you know. And of course, there were his friends. Men friends.
CALLAN:	You one of them?
RITCHIE:	I? Good Lord, no. I was scarcely presentable enough for Gerald.
CALLAN:	You're on the photograph.
RITCHIE:	We were at school together. He was a very dominating boy and one did not grudge his domination. He was Prince Hamlet and I an attending lord.
CALLAN:	And the other chap?
RITCHIE:	Oddly enough, when one considers my calling, his name was Bishop.
CALLAN:	First name?
RITCHIE: *(Sly)*	Christian name?
CALLAN: *(Shrugs)*	Ah.
RITCHIE:	Ian. A bad influence, I thought.
CALLAN:	On Sir Gerald?
RITCHIE:	Certainly not on me. I had already decided on my way of life. Bishop was a degenerate. Need I say more?

CALLAN:	Not yet. And not to me.
RITCHIE:	I shall be questioned by others?
CALLAN:	Maybe. You haven't given me much.
RITCHIE:	I was never Bishop's intimate. All I remember is that he flattered Gerald disgracefully. That made him pompous. I dislike pomposity. But he did encourage Gerald in entering the Civil Service as a scientist. They took a trip abroad together, I remember, just before Gerald joined his department. That would be 1936. Bishop never came back.
CALLAN:	Where did they go?
RITCHIE:	Gerald was evasive on the subject and I lost touch. My vocation took me far away from the seats of the mighty. I never saw Gerald again in the flesh. But in the newspapers, magazines, even on television. How well Gerald has done.
CALLAN:	You're not jealous?
RITCHIE:	Dullness is agreeable to me. I'm quite happy as an attendant lord, Mr Callan.
CALLAN:	I see. I don't think I need keep you any further.
RITCHIE:	No. There is one more thing.
CALLAN:	I thought perhaps there might be.
RITCHIE:	You're much too shrewd for a poor parson. The year that Gerald and his friend went abroad...
CALLAN:	1936?
RITCHIE:	That was the year that the Spanish Civil War broke out. I have often wondered if there was any connection between the two events: the one so trivial, the other cataclysmic.
CALLAN:	Have you any evidence?
RITCHIE:	Inference merely. Benson might help.
CALLAN:	Who's Benson?
RITCHIE:	Another friend of Bishop's. They were at the same college. He lives in London, I believe. Roger Benson, he's in the book.
CALLAN:	I'll look him up.
RITCHIE:	I should take a bottle of whisky. He drinks a great deal.
CALLAN:	Most useful.

(CALLAN moves towards the desk, eyeing the typewriter)

It's in marvellous nick.

RITCHIE:	
(Confused)	Nick?
CALLAN:	Condition.
RITCHIE:	It has to be on my stipend.
CALLAN:	You don't mind if I try it out?

(CALLAN moves behind the desk, sits down and feeds a sheet of paper into the typewriter. He types rapidly, ignoring RITCHIE.)

RITCHIE: Well, really...It is a most delicate instrument.

CALLAN:

(Pulling sheet of paper out and handing it to RITCHIE)

And deadly too.

RITCHIE:	
(Reading)	Sir Gerald is a Communist traitor. His sexual activities are disgusting.
CALLAN:	Somebody else typed that.
RITCHIE:	Indeed?
CALLAN:	Yeah. Then they took a day off, went up to London and delivered it by hand. You go up to London, do you, sir?
RITCHIE:	What makes you think so?
CALLAN:	You've seen Benson, haven't you?
RITCHIE:	One likes to keep in touch.
CALLAN:	And stir up a little mud.
RITCHIE:	You can prove that this other message was done on my typewriter?
CALLAN:	Easiest thing in the world. Your bishop wouldn't like that, would he?
RITCHIE:	
(Bristling)	It was my patriotic duty.
CALLAN:	He still wouldn't like it.
RITCHIE:	No. No he would not.
CALLAN:	No he wouldn't. We can rely on your discretion then, can't we?

(RITCHIE nods sadly, defeated, but says nothing.)

And no more muck-raking, please. Just go on being dull, Reverend.

INT. HUNTER'S OFFICE. DAY.

(CALLAN and HUNTER prowling around the office. Between them, slumped

159

	and dishevelled in a chair is a third man – BENSON, who at first seems unconscious but slowly begins to stir.)
CALLAN:	He's coming round.
HUNTER:	Better open another bottle.
	(HUNTER walks casually around the seated man whilst CALLAN takes a bottle of whisky from a desk draw and opens it, pouring a very large measure into a glass on the desk as HUNTER speaks.)
	He was very promising, you know. Just missed a Fellowship. Worked for some first rate magazines. Wrote a brilliant book. He never actually joined the party. He was much too subtle for them anyway. But he felt things very deeply. Perhaps that's why...
	(BENSON stirs and CALLAN goes to him. Gently shakes his shoulder.)
CALLAN:	Alright, old chap? Come on, old chap. How you feeling?
BENSON:	
(Confused)	Passed out, did I? Trouble is I don't get enough. I can't afford to really, with Scotch the price it is.
	(HUNTER picks up the full glass of whisky and holds it out. As Benson reaches for it, HUNTER nods to CALLAN.)
CALLAN:	We were talking about Ian Bishop.
BENSON:	Who? I'm sorry, my mind's not always...
	(CALLAN picks up a photograph from the desk and shows it to him.)
CALLAN:	This chap.
BENSON:	Spain, 1936. They were both there – in Barcelona.
	(HUNTER gives him the glass and BENSON drinks greedily before continuing.)
	Naylor didn't stay. But Ian – he was in my battalion of the International Brigade for a bit.
CALLAN:	Was he killed?
BENSON:	In a way. We all died in Spain, old man.
HUNTER:	
(Sharp)	Cut out the journalism, Benson.
BENSON:	No. He wasn't killed.

(CALLAN reaches over with the whisky bottle and fills BENSON's now empty glass as he speaks.)

He was taken off – for special duties.

CALLAN: Who by?

BENSON: The Russians, old man. When it was special duties it was always the Russians. He was taken back to Russia.

CALLAN: Why?

BENSON:
(Shrugging)

For training?

CALLAN: What kind of training?

BENSON:
(Dramatic)

The overthrow of capitalism! That was what everybody trained for. Ian was attractive. I expect they would use that. And he was very brave, you know. The way I tried to be. Why do you want to know about him?

HUNTER: About who?

BENSON: Why, Ian Bishop.

HUNTER: I've never heard of him.

(To CALLAN:) Have you?

CALLAN: Never heard of him.

HUNTER: Come on old chap, drink up.

BENSON:
(Confused)

But you showed me his picture...

HUNTER: What picture? There's no picture.

BENSON:
(Drifting off)

Didn't he...?

(BENSON passes out. HUNTER leans over him to check he is not faking, then turns to CALLAN.)

HUNTER: Take him out and ditch him. Better take a car.

CALLAN: Won't he talk?

HUNTER: Who would believe him? He won't even believe himself.

CALLAN: Can I go back to Naylor?

(HUNTER nods agreement then takes a small tape-recorder from a desk drawer and hands it to CALLAN.)

HUNTER: Get the truth out of him, Callan, all of it. I'll make you an appointment for 4.30.

CALLAN: Right.

(He points to the slumped BENSON)

Where does he go?

> *(HUNTER takes some notes from his
> wallet and stuffs them into the breast
> pocket of BENSON's jacket.)*

HUNTER: Outside a pub, Callan, any pub. Notting Hill if you're feeling kind. He has a room there.

> *(CALLAN picks up a hat from under the
> chair and unceremoniously crams it on
> to BENSON's head. BENSON does not stir.)*

INT. LONELY'S FLAT. DAY

> *(FX: distant traffic, children playing. LONELY
> opens door of his flat as CALLAN knocks.)*

CALLAN:
(SOV) Lonely?

LONELY:
(Opening door) Mr Callan. Is there anything you want, Mr Callan?

CALLAN: Why should I?

LONELY: Well, I don't know, do I?

CALLAN: No, Lonely. This is a social call.

LONELY: You never made no social calls before.

CALLAN: I know. It's very remiss of me. But most of the time I'm busy. You're getting as bit like that.

LONELY: How d'you mean?

CALLAN: I needed you last night.

LONELY: Mr Callan, I told you...

CALLAN: Yes...I nearly got nicked last night.

LONELY:
(Shocked) You never.

CALLAN: I needed a look-out last night.

LONELY:
(Squirming) Mr Callan, I had to get three hundred quid.

CALLAN: *(Pulling up a
chair and sitting)* What did you need it for?

LONELY: It's money, isn't it?

CALLAN:
(Reasonable) What d'you need it for? If you'd said it was for a bird or something...

LONELY:
(Shocked) Me? Three hundred quid for a bird?

CALLAN: *(Stands up
suddenly, right in
LONELY's face)* Then what did you get it for? Now look,

162

you and me don't have any secrets do we? What's it for?

LONELY:
(Pleading)

Mr Callan, I daren't. He'll hurt me. He's got friends. They take you down to a garage and they do things to you. Electric shocks and that. He wants me to do another job tonight to get the money.

CALLAN:

Who?

LONELY:
(Panic)

He's got me scared. I can't work proper. He's putting the block on me, Mr Callan.

CALLAN:
(Angry)

Who?

LONELY:

I screwed a drum a few months back. I didn't know where it was. Honest. I got near a thousand quid's worth of stuff. Turned out to be Big Mike Kennedy's. You've heard of him?

CALLAN:

I've heard of him.

LONELY:

If he knew I screwed his drum he'd half kill me. And this git says he'll tell him. And he can prove it. He's got Big Mike's lighter.

CALLAN:

What?

LONELY:

Well, I had to sell some of the stuff... What am I going to do, Mr Callan?

CALLAN:
(Grim)
(LONELY remains silent)

Who is this git?

Lonely, I'm the only chance you've got. Who is he?

LONELY:

Todd. That's the only name I know. I've already given him £200 and he's coming for the other £300 tomorrow.

CALLAN:

I'll tell you what to do. You nip off to the off-licence, come back here and stop worrying.

LONELY:

But he's coming here this evening at six o'clock to tell me where the job is.

CALLAN:

Maybe he'll see me instead.

LONELY:

What'll you do to him, Mr Callan?

CALLAN:

I'll get him off your back, son.

LONELY:

But his mates...

CALLAN:

When I've finished with him he won't have any mates.

LONELY:

He's a real bad 'un, Mr Callan.

CALLAN:

Is he? In your considered opinion is he as bad as me?

(Close up on LONELY's reaction as he thinks this through but is not sure how to answer.)

163

Come on, get off to the boozer and treat yourself.
(CALLAN takes out wallet and offers notes)

LONELY:
(Taking the money,
but cautious)   You'll wait for me, Mr Callan?
(CALLAN nods.)

INT. NAYLOR'S STUDY. DAY

{FX: phone rings. NAYLOR answers it)

NAYLOR: Sir Gerald Naylor.
OPERATOR:
(SOV)   Sir Gerald Naylor? A Mr Ian is calling you from Berlin and wishes you to pay for the call. Will you accept the charge?
NAYLOR: Ian? Yes, alright. Put him on.
OPERATOR:
(SOV)   Sir Gerald will pay for the call. Go ahead please.

BISHOP:
(V/O)   *Danke schön, Fraulein.* So you recognised 'Mr Ian' did you, love?
NAYLOR: Of course I did. But what are you doing in West Berlin?

BISHOP:
(V/O)   Drinking excellent beer and listening to terrible music. What else can one do in West Berlin? Actually, I'm on my way to see you.
NAYLOR: That's marvellous.
BISHOP:
(V/O)   I think so too, Gerry. I've missed you.
NAYLOR: Have you?
BISHOP:
(V/O)   I really have.
NAYLOR: How soon am I going to see you?
BISHOP:
(V/O)   Tomorrow, 12.30. At Franchi's. They tell me it's still there.
NAYLOR: Yes it is. But I haven't been since...
BISHOP:
(V/O)   You really are a love, Gerry. And I treated you awfully badly. I had to. You know that. Are you going to do what I asked you?
NAYLOR: Yes.

BISHOP:
(V/O)
NAYLOR:
BISHOP:
(V/O)

I knew you would.
Did you, Ian?

Of course. It isn't spying at all, you see. It's preserving world peace. And you want that almost as much as you want your wife, don't you, love? 12.30 tomorrow. Franchi's. Don't write it down.
(Close up on NAYLOR'S face as he replaces the receiver.)

END OF PART TWO

INT. NAYLOR'S FLAT. DAY.

*(NAYLOR and CALLAN
confronting each other.)*

NAYLOR: Really, Mr Callan, I can see no point in going on with these conversations.

CALLAN: Can't you?

NAYLOR: Either I'm guilty or I'm not.

CALLAN: That's right.

NAYLOR: And you've no proof of my guilt. Obviously, because it doesn't exist.

*(CALLAN moves casually to the
desk and picks up and opens
the cigarette box.)*

CALLAN: That's a nice cigarette box.

NAYLOR: Yes.

CALLAN:
(Reading inscription) G' is for Gerald I suppose? And the 'I'... what's the 'I' for?

NAYLOR: Just someone I used to know.

CALLAN: A girl?

NAYLOR: Yes. A girl.

CALLAN: What was her name?

NAYLOR: Iris.

CALLAN:
(Sarcastic) Yes. There aren't a lot beginning with 'I' are there?

*(CALLAN opens the secret drawer in
the bottom of the box and produces
the photograph. He holds it
out, feigning surprise.)*

NAYLOR: May I see that? Good Lord, I wonder how that got in there? I haven't seen that photograph for twenty-five years. Those were two men I was at Cambridge with, you know.

CALLAN: Yes.

NAYLOR: The chap with the punt-pole became a parson or something. I've quite forgotten who the other one was. Ah well, I shan't need it again. No point in hanging on to old memories for too long.

166

CALLAN:	No point at all.
NAYLOR:	It's far better to get rid of them, don't you think?
	(NAYLOR tears up the picture and drops the pieces into an ash-tray on the desk, then produces a box of matches, lights one and burns the picture. CALLAN waits until the smoke has wafted away, then reaches into an inside pocket and produces a wedge of pictures.)
CALLAN:	Far better. Would you like to burn these too? We took quite a lot of copies, you know.
NAYLOR:	But where did you...? Nobody has another copy only...
CALLAN:	Only Ian. The 'I' stands for Ian, doesn't it? And we couldn't get his, could we? This one is yours, Sir Gerald.
NAYLOR: *(Outraged)*	You broke into my flat?
CALLAN:	Yes.
NAYLOR:	But I showed you everything.
CALLAN:	Everything except this. Why did you hide this?
NAYLOR: *(Blustering)*	You committed an offence!
CALLAN:	Do you want to take me to court?
NAYLOR: *(Deflated)*	No. It's not important.
CALLAN:	I noticed when you burned that picture your hands were shaking. Was it hard to hurt him?
NAYLOR:	I don't understand you. A picture of an undergraduate who went into the Church? As I remember he was rather malicious.
CALLAN:	This one still is.
NAYLOR:	Oh my God.
CALLAN:	It's the other boy I want to talk about. But he'll be a man now, won't he? About your age.
NAYLOR:	A year younger.
CALLAN:	You went to Spain with him, didn't you?
NAYLOR:	A lot of people went to Spain. It was like a crusade. The forces of light against the forces of darkness.
CALLAN:	And the forces of darkness won.
NAYLOR:	No. The imagery doesn't hold. I was 21 years old, Mr Callan. Everyone over-

167

	simplifies at that age. I see things quite differently nowadays, I promise you. And yet, do you know, I'm glad I did it. I fought for what was right. Surely that is something to be proud of.
CALLAN:	Except that you kept it hidden. You never once admitted that you'd fought in Spain.
NAYLOR:	My masters would hardly consider it an advantage in my career.
CALLAN:	And does your wife know?
NAYLOR:	No. For Ruth, Spain is a place where one acquires a tan in summer. My war was over when she was two years old.
CALLAN:	Was it?
NAYLOR:	Yes.

(They both react as LADY NAYLOR (RUTH) enters.)

RUTH:	Darling, I don't want to disturb you... Oh, good evening Mr...?
NAYLOR:	Callan. What is it, Ruth?
RUTH:	You won't forget that we're dining with the Felthams, will you?
NAYLOR:	No, I won't forget.
RUTH:	Because if you're going to be delayed I really ought to phone them.
CALLAN:	

(Before NAYLOR can say anything)

I think you should, Lady Naylor.

RUTH: *(Annoyed)*	Really, Gerald, they're absolutely relying on us.
NAYLOR:	I'll be there.
CALLAN:	Sir Gerald, I honestly don't think you'll be able to go, not even when we've finished.
RUTH:	Gerald, is everything alright?
NAYLOR:	Yes, yes...Mr Callan and I have to go over something which he considers important.
RUTH:	Don't you?
NAYLOR:	To me the whole thing is immensely trivial. Would you like a drink, Mr Callan?
CALLAN:	Yes I would, please. Straight Scotch.
NAYLOR:	I think I'll join you. You, my dear?
RUTH:	No thank you. Mr Callan, what's wrong?
CALLAN:	I'm afraid this one is most secret, Lady Naylor.
RUTH:	You seem to have got my husband worried.
CALLAN:	I've got a lot of people worried. It's my job.

RUTH:	But my husband isn't just anybody, you know.
CALLAN:	Yes. Yes, I do know.
RUTH:	That's what I'm saying.
NAYLOR:	And the more important you are the more you have to worry.
CALLAN:	Exactly. That's why I never worry.
RUTH:	
(Staring hard at CALLAN)	I think you worry all the time.

INT. SECTION H.Q. EVENING

(HUNTER sitting at his desk is reading from a file and speaking into the intercom.)

HUNTER: Height five eleven, weight about ten stone, grey eyes. According to Benson he has a scar on his left index finger. Nothing dramatic, something to do with a tin-opener. I think it may be the chap who did those jobs in Teheran in the Forties. Could you check? Accent, pure Cambridge. His real name is Ian Bishop, if that helps at all and this is most urgent please. With any luck he may be coming to visit us quite soon, cheeky young pup.

INT. NAYLOR'S FLAT. EVENING

(As NAYLOR ushers his wife out of the room, CALLAN sets up a portable tape-recorder on the desk.)

NAYLOR: If you'll excuse us, my dear, we really must get on.

RUTH: I'd better call Mrs Feltham.

NAYLOR: Yes, perhaps you'd better do that.
(RUTH leaves and NAYLOR closes the door behind her then turns back to look at CALLAN and sips from the glass of Scotch he is holding.)

CALLAN: You love her very much?

NAYLOR: Of course.

CALLAN: She's a lot younger than you.

NAYLOR: That's none of your business.

CALLAN: I'm afraid it is. We did a bit of homework
            on her too. Brought up very strictly,
            wasn't she?
NAYLOR: I happen to be very fond of her parents.
CALLAN: Yes I'm sure. They couldn't give her much,
            could they? Except a fear of Hellfire. Now
            you can give her everything: nice car, posh
            flat, a title. Just before you got married
            you even came into money. In a way, you
            could say you bought her.
NAYLOR: You...

            *(NAYLOR throws the contents of his
            glass at CALLAN, who dodges and
            comes at NAYLOR fast, smashing the
            glass from NAYLOR's hand. CALLAN
            pushes him violently down into a chair.)*

CALLAN: Right. I want you to listen to something.
            *(CALLAN turns back to the desk and
            turns the tape-recorder on. The voices heard
            are those of BENSON and CALLAN.)*

BENSON:
(SOV)   He was taken back to Russia.
CALLAN:
(SOV)   Why?
BENSON:
(SOV)   For training.
CALLAN:
(SOV)   What kind of training?
BENSON:
(SOV)   The overthrow of capitalism, that's what
            everybody was trained for. Ian was
            attractive. I expect they would use that.
            (CALLAN stops the tape.)

CALLAN:
(Quoting) 'Ian was attractive. I expect they would
            use that.'
NAYLOR: Say it all, Callan. I want to get it over.
CALLAN: Right. The big love of your life was Ian
            Bishop. Until she came along. Suppose
            she ever found out?
NAYLOR: You wouldn't tell her...
CALLAN: Hasn't he threatened to?
            (NAYLOR's head drops)

            Shall I tell you what I think? I think he
            contacted you, asked after your wife, told
            you all you had to do was co-operate and
            she need never know. I bet he told you

            170

something else too. I bet he said you wouldn't be spying at all. Not really, you'd be helping world peace.

NAYLOR: How on Earth did you...

CALLAN: They always do, Sir Gerald. Well?

NAYLOR: You might have been listening.

CALLAN: I'll tell you what you are. You're what we call in the trade a 'sleeper'. To them you've been in a deep-freeze since 1936. And then it was time they thawed you out. When you got married and you got the job they wanted you to get.

NAYLOR: He still had all my letters, you see. He said he'd show them to Ruth. I can't lose Ruth, Callan. Not now.

CALLAN: Perhaps you won't have to, if we pick him up. When's he coming to see you?

NAYLOR: He said tomorrow, unless I warned him off.

CALLAN: Have you?

(NAYLOR shakes his head)

That should be a help then.

(FX: phone ringing. NAYLOR goes to answer it.)

NAYLOR: Sir Gerald Naylor.

HUNTER:
(SOV) Mr Callan, please.

(NAYLOR hands the receiver silently to CALLAN.)

CALLAN: Thank you. Callan.

HUNTER:
(SOV) Charlie here. How's it going?

CALLAN: Bishop's visiting our friend tomorrow.

HUNTER:
(SOV) And you'll be in attendance?

CALLAN: Yes.

CUT To: INT. HUNTER'S OFFICE.

(HUNTER on phone to CALLAN)

HUNTER: Good. Bishop's been something of a blister in the past. Teheran, Iraq, the Lebanon. The Englishman Abroad, you know. He could tell us a great deal, very useful stuff.

171

CALLAN:
(SOV)
HUNTER:

That's a help then.
And the patient? Should we let him go to
the Dominions?

CUT BACK TO INT. NAYLOR'S FLAT

(CALLAN on phone)

CALLAN:
HUNTER:
(SOV)
CALLAN:
HUNTER:
(SOV)
CALLAN:

No.

Really? I thought you liked him.
I do.

Well then?
He's too vulnerable.

(NAYLOR reacts with surprise.)

HUNTER:

Forthcoming was he?

CUT BACK TO INT. HUNTER'S OFFICE.

(HUNTER nodding into phone)

HUNTER:

Yes. I see what you mean. Come in soon.
Charlie's longing to hear all about it.

CUT BACK TO INT. NAYLOR'S FLAT.

(CALLAN hangs up the phone)

NAYLOR:
CALLAN:
NAYLOR:

CALLAN:

NAYLOR:

Well?
I'm not recommending you.
But you'll get hold of Ian and he's the only
one. I swear.
I'm sorry. You can be hurt too easily. I
really am sorry.
You know, when I heard from Ian the
other day I realised something. I still love
him very much. And look what I've done
to him, so that I could keep the love of the
only other human being I ever cared for.
And now I shall lose her too.

172

	(CALLAN wanders casually across the room to the study door. Suddenly he leaps forward and whips the door open to reveal RUTH.)
CALLAN:	Come in, Lady Naylor.
	(RUTH pushes by CALLAN and rushes to confront her husband)
RUTH:	We're not going to Canada are we?
CALLAN: *(To NAYLOR)*	She listened on the extension.
RUTH:	It's true isn't it? We're not going.
CALLAN:	No. You're not going. Your husband's going to be ill. They'll have to send somebody else. When he's better, they'll find him another job.
RUTH:	But not Canada?
CALLAN:	No, not Canada.
RUTH:	But why not? Tell me. I've got a right to know. What did he do?
CALLAN:	You're his wife. You should be on his side. What makes you think he did anything?
RUTH:	Because you're here.
CALLAN:	Alright, I've hurt him. It's my job. It isn't yours. We haven't finished yet, would you mind waiting outside?
	(RUTH glares at her husband, who remains silent. CALLAN insists.)
	Please...
	(RUTH leaves. CALLAN closes the door behind her and turns back to confront NAYLOR)
	Right. When and where are you meeting Bishop?
NAYLOR:	12.30. We're having lunch together in Franchi's in Soho. We used to eat there in the Thirties.
CALLAN:	We'll be there too. You'll be watched from now on.
NAYLOR:	Yes, I thought I might be.
	(CALLAN collects the tape recorder and the photographs from the desk.)
CALLAN:	I'll be off, Sir Gerald. You've had enough for one day.
NAYLOR:	Goodbye.
	(CALLAN leaves the room, but RUTH is in the doorway waiting to re-enter.)

173

CALLAN:	'Night, Lady Naylor.
NAYLOR: *(Shouting after CALLAN as he exits)*	
	Mr Callan, you'll recognise Ian quite easily tomorrow. He's the one I shall greet as a very old, dear friend.
(RUTH replaces CALLAN in front of NAYLOR)	
	Ruth, my darling. I realise that this will take a great deal of explanation...
RUTH:	Don't talk! For God's sake, don't talk. Oh, you fool, you stupid old fool.

INT. LONELY'S FLAT. EVENING.

(FX: distant traffic and a clock on the mantle piece ticking loudly. LONELY keeps glancing nervously at the clock.)

LONELY: Oh, come on, Mr Callan. Please get here. Please.

EXT. OUTSIDE LONELY'S FLAT.

(A car driven by TODD draws up. As TODD switches off the engine, CALLAN pulls open the passenger door and climbs in.)

CALLAN:	Good evening, squire.
TODD:	What the hell do you think you're doing? If you don't get out of this car I'll...
CALLAN:	Call the police? Will you really? There's one down the road now. If you yell hard enough he'll hear you. What I really came in here for was to show you something.
TODD:	What?
	(CALLAN pulls his gun from his shoulder holster and levels it at TODD)
CALLAN:	This.
TODD:	You're crazy.
CALLAN:	It's the crazy ones who pull the trigger. Do something for me?
TODD:	What?
CALLAN:	Take me for a drive.
TODD:	If you're that tough friend of Lonely's, I better warn you. I've got tough friends too.

174

CALLAN: If I were you, I'd start to drive, mate. Otherwise I might just go off you. Know what I mean?

(TODD drives as directed by CALLAN through darkening streets until CALLAN indicates that they turn into a deserted alley. The car comes to a halt and the lights are turned off. Inside the car, CALLAN brandishes his gun in TODD's face.)

CALLAN: Alright – out.
TODD:
*(Hands gripping the
steering wheel tightly)*   No.

(CALLAN swipes TODD across the face with the barrel of his gun.)

CALLAN: You can walk or I can carry you. Make up your mind.

(TODD gets out of the car as CALLAN, covering him with the gun, gets out his side. CALLAN waves the gun to force TODD down the dark alley.)

CALLAN: Move. Go on, move. Turn your back. Go on, right round. Good boy. Go on, move. Good boy.

(TODD stumbles down the alley, his hands up, CALLAN holding the gun on him until he comes to a dead end and stands facing the brick wall. Behind him, CALLAN puts the gun back in his shoulder-holster, makes a fist and punches TODD in the kidneys. As TODD doubles up in pain, CALLAN continues to give him a savage beating. When TODD is unconscious and on the ground, CALLAN straightens up, brushes off his jacket and trousers and looks down at TODD.)

CALLAN: Oh mate, you've got a lot to learn about handling yourself.

INT. RESTAURANT. DAY.

(BISHOP is sitting at a table drinking a glass of wine, with another glass in front of him. CALLAN is seen at another table, but paying no attention to BISHOP. He only looks round when

	NAYLOR enters the restaurant and makes his way over to BISHOP.)
NAYLOR:	Ian...
(CALLAN looks away)	Hello, love. Your drink's all ready.
	(NAYLOR sits down and BISHOP reaches out to touch his hand on the table. NAYLOR picks up the glass on the table, swirls it around.)
NAYLOR:	Just the way I like it. You haven't forgotten.
BISHOP:	Not about you, Gerry. I never forget a thing about you.
NAYLOR:	It's been the same with me.
BISHOP:	Has it, love? I'm glad. I didn't want to...force you, you know.
NAYLOR:	I know.
BISHOP:	And your wife will never know now, I promise you.
	(CALLAN stands up as do two other Section men. Whilst they cover the exits, CALLAN moves to the table where BISHOP and NAYLOR sit.)
CALLAN:	Your car's ready, Mr Bishop.
BISHOP:	
(Head turning sharply)	I'm afraid you've made a mistake. My name's not Bishop.
	(The two Section operatives move closer)
CALLAN:	Be sociable, sir. We don't want a scene do we?
BISHOP:	Certainly not.
(To NAYLOR)	We never had scenes at Franchi's in the old days. Did you tell them, Gerry?
NAYLOR: *(Sad)*	Yes.
BISHOP:	Poor love. What have we done to you?
CALLAN:	Come on, Sir Gerald. I've got a cab waiting to take you home.
NAYLOR:	
(Rising slowly to go with CALLAN)	Not to my home. To my flat, Mr Callan. A home is where one's wife is. And my wife left me last night.
	(NAYLOR looks CALLAN in the eye but CALLAN remains impassive)
	You've taken everything I ever had.
	(CALLAN escorts him out of the restaurant.)

END CREDITS